THE CASTLE OF OLLADA

Gothic Classics

The Castle of Ollada

by

Francis Lathom

Edited with an introduction and notes by
James D. Jenkins

CHICAGO
VALANCOURT BOOKS
MMVI

Published by Valancourt Books
Chicago, Illinois

First published in 1795

First published by Valancourt Books, February 2005
New edition, February 2006

Introduction and notes © 2006 James D. Jenkins
Cover design by Ryan Cagle

The Castle of Ollada
ISBN 0-9766048-2-5
Library of Congress Control Number: 2005921988

Printed in the United States of America

CONTENTS

INTRODUCTION

Francis Lathom, as was justly remarked by Montague Summers in *The Gothic Quest* (1938), was in many ways one of the most interesting as well as one of the most typical of the minor Gothic novelists.

Summers gives a brief account of Lathom's life, which for many years represented the only biographical information on Lathom; unfortunately, however, it is almost entirely a mixture of inaccuracy and surmise. Summers, drawing mainly on the entry on Lathom in the *Dictionary of National Biography*, tells us, for example, that Lathom was born in 1777 at Norwich, and that he was rumoured to have been the illegitimate son of an English peer. At some point, Summers writes, Lathom left Norwich for rural Scotland. The "secret" behind this unusual relocation, Summers informs us (without citing any evidence), is that Lathom was homosexual and chose to accompany a lover to Scotland. The rest of the story, in a nutshell, is that Lathom lived as a lodger in Aberdeenshire on the farm of one Alexander Rennie, where he abruptly died in 1832. Summers embellishes his account, portraying Lathom as fond of Scotch whisky, dressing oddly, reading the London papers and entertaining the local villagers with songs of his own composition.

Whether some of the details provided by Summers and the *Dictionary of National Biography* are true or not may never be learned; however, my own recent research suggests that much of it is false.

Lathom was, in fact, born not in 1777 at Norwich, but in July 1774 at Rotterdam, Holland.[1] He was christened there at the English Episcopal Church on July 14. Lathom's father, Henry, was a merchant involved in trade with the East India Company, a commerce in which he was apparently abundantly successful. Henry Lathom was originally a native of Norwich and married Francis's mother Sarah Hussey at Norwich's St. George Colegate church in May 1772. It seems nearly impossible that Francis Lathom could have been the illegitimate son of an English peer (as has very often been alleged, perhaps because it lends added intrigue to his history) unless the peripatetic nobleman happened to show up in East Anglia in time to impregnate Sarah before she left for Rotterdam with Henry, or unless this mysterious lord had also relocated to Holland.

The Lathoms apparently resided at Rotterdam for some time, since Henry Lathom in his 1813 will refers to himself as "formerly of Rotterdam," which suggests longer than a transitory stay there.[2] Henry obviously did quite well in his trade; Francis undoubtedly had his father's success in mind when he wrote in *Men and Manners*

(1799) that "Mr. Hutchinbunck...heard of the fortunes amassed by English merchants in Holland...[and] contrived to buy his passage to Rotterdam."

The Lathoms returned to the Norwich area at some point, perhaps in 1777, which would help explain the erroneous conjecture that Francis was born there in that year. The family took up residence in Catton, outside the city of Norwich, but moved within the city limits by 1795.[3]

Young Francis was early drawn to the theatre and was fortunate to live near the Theatre Royal Norwich, the largest theatre in England outside London and known as a "rich recruiting ground for Covent Garden and Drury-Lane."[4] Before he had completed his eighteenth year, Lathom had already begun penning comedies and light farces for the Norwich stage.

Known today chiefly for his novels, Francis Lathom's success as a minor playwright has unfortunately been greatly underestimated.[5] His first published play, *All in a Bustle* (1795), was popular enough to run into a second edition in 1800. *The Dash of the Day* (1800) met with even greater success, for it was performed to "universal applause," and ran into at least three editions at Norwich, as well as a reprint at Dublin in 1801. Although there is no evidence Lathom's plays were acted at the larger London theatres,[6] he was apparently known there, for his *Orlando and Seraphina*, "an heroic drama" was published at London in 1800, as was his *Curiosity* (1801), an adaptation of a French work by Madame de Genlis, which was generally agreed to surpass the quality of the original.[7] *Holiday Time, or the Schoolboy's Frolic* (1800) was printed at Norwich, but according the title page, could also be had "in London of Messrs. Longman and Rees...and of one bookseller in every principal town of the Kingdom." The manuscript of an 1802 play entitled *The Fools of Fashion*, which has been attributed to Lathom, survives in the Larpent Collection of the Huntington Library in California; that it was never performed or published may be partially explained by the fact that Lathom apparently left Norwich around this time (as will be discussed later). His final published play, *The Wife of a Million*, a comedy in five acts (1803), apparently met with the most widespread popularity, being performed not only at Norwich, but also at provincial theatres at Lincoln and Canterbury.

Young Lathom, however, did not limit himself to the writing of dramas; he tried his hand at penning a romance with *The Castle of Ollada*, published in two volumes at William Lane's Minerva Press in 1795. *The Castle of Ollada*, issued a year after *The Mysteries of*

Udolpho, apparently met with success from a reading public still en-
amoured of Gothic romances in the style of Ann Radcliffe.

By the age of twenty-one, Lathom had become something of a
minor local celebrity. The son of a wealthy merchant and the author
of a Gothic romance and at least one popular comedy, Lathom was off
to a brilliant start in his life and career.

In 1797 he married Diana Ganning, the daughter of the wealthy
Norwich attorney and landowner Daniel Ganning.[8] Diana Ganning's
will of 1851 refers to a trust consisting of funds from the marriage
settlement, and it may be presumed that Daniel Ganning, who died in
1809 possessed of numerous land holdings and more than £25,000 in
cash, must have paid a very handsome dowry to Francis Lathom.

The following year, Lathom published the book that was to en-
sure his literary immortality—even if only as a footnote—*The Midnight Bell.* This novel proved extremely popular and was translated
into French as *La Cloche de minuit* (1799) and adapted for the Gothic
chapbook market as *The Midnight Bell, or The Abbey of St. Francis*
(1800). The novel's enduring memory is owing to no less a writer
than Jane Austen, who singled out *The Midnight Bell* as one of the
seven "horrid novels" named in *Northanger Abbey* (1818).[9]

Curiously, Lathom did not follow the success of his two Gothic
romances with another novel in the same style; rather, in 1799 he
published *Men and Manners,* a satire of contemporary life. Summers
claimed this novel ran into four editions, although only three survive
today (the London and Dublin editions of 1799 and an edition of
1800, which is unhelpfully labelled a "new edition.") Summers called
the book Lathom's masterpiece and wrote that its well-drawn and
humorous characters were worthy of a young Dickens.

The same year as Lathom's greatest literary success to date, the
Lathom household enjoyed another blessing in 1799, their son Henry
Daniel being born on April 8 of that year. The couple would go on to
have two more children, Frederick, born in 1800, and Jessy Ann,
born in 1803.

The first year of the nineteenth century saw publication of
Lathom's *Mystery* (1800), a very strange blend of a domestic episto-
lary novel with shocking Gothic horror. Lathom did not publish any
novels in 1801, although he continued to write for the Norwich theatre, where, if the *Dictionary of National Biography* can be believed,
he also acted. Presumably during these years Lathom divided his
time between his theatrical pursuits and the rearing of his two infant
children.

At some point during this period, Lathom left Norwich. Summers asserts that it was in 1802 or 1803, and although he gives no

support for this statement, he is probably correct.[10] Lathom's last child, Jessy Ann, was born in July 1803, which suggests that he resided in Norwich at least until her conception, which must have occurred around October 1802. The probable departure of Lathom from Norwich in late 1802 or early 1803 is further confirmed by the fact that his 1802 play *The Fools of Fashion* remained unpublished, while his *The Wife of a Million*, supposed to be written in 1802, was the last of his works to be published at Norwich, in 1803.

The reason why Francis Lathom left the city in which he had enjoyed such great success as a playwright and novelist, the city where his aged mother and father still resided and where he inhabited a house with his wife and children, is still unknown. Montague Summers, as was mentioned above, conjectured it involved a gay love affair. Although there is no evidence of this, neither can it be wholly discounted, especially considering the homosexual subtexts which run through many of Lathom's works.

Whatever it was that caused Lathom to leave Norwich for Scotland, it must have been fairly serious. When his father Henry died in 1812, he left a five page will which devotes only about half a page to his only son Francis. This very singular will bequeaths to Francis "a yearly sum of two hundred pounds by equal half yearly payments" but only "on the express condition that [Francis...] relinquish [...] as far as by law he can or may the custody care and guardianship of Henry Frederick and Jessy Ann Lathom the three adolescent children of my said son Francis by Diana his wife and shall permit them and any of them during their respective minorities to be wholly and entirely under the direction and management of their mother and [...] shall not in any way or manner whatever assert controul or interfere in or with the [...] bringing up of the said three children."[11] The will goes on to specify that if Lathom did not comply with this unusual condition, his annuity would cease. Diana, for her part, reverted to her maiden name and changed the children's names from Lathom to Ganning.

Why would Henry Lathom demand that his son stay away from his own wife and children? It could very well be, as Summers suggested, that Lathom was forced into exile after a gay sex scandal. But it is also possible that, in a city as charged with political and religious discord as Norwich was in the late 1790s, the cause of Lathom's departure from Norwich resulted from a falling-out over politics or religion. Indeed, whatever Lathom may have done to occasion his exile from Norwich, there are nearly unlimited possibilities to explain it.

Whatever may have caused Lathom's departure from Norwich, what cannot be disputed is that the years after his removal were among the most productive of his career. The year 1803 saw publication of two translations, *The Castle of the Tuileries*, from a French work by Pierre Joseph Alexis Roussel, and *Erestina*, from Marie-Jeanne Riccoboni's *Ernestine*. Also in 1803 Lathom published perhaps the most humorous of all his works, *Very Strange, But Very True!*, a farcical novel in four volumes.

During the first five or six years after quitting Norwich, Lathom also published *The Impenetrable Secret, Find it Out!* (1805), *The Mysterious Freebooter* (1806), *Human Beings* (1807), *The Fatal Vow* (1807), *The Unknown* (1808), *London, or Truth Without Treason* (1809), and *The Romance of the Hebrides* (1809).

Among these, *The Impenetrable Secret* and *The Fatal Vow* can be singled out as fine, but minor, Gothic romances. *The Mysterious Freebooter*, however, was an extraordinary success, running into a third edition by 1829 and reprinted as late as 1844. Arthur Alastair MacConochie, one of Lathom's very few critics, cited *The Mysterious Freebooter* as one of the earliest examples of authentic historical fiction in English, predating Sir Walter Scott's *Waverly* (1814) by eight years.

The Fatal Vow and *The Unknown* followed *The Mysterious Freebooter* in the vein of the historical Gothic. *The Fatal Vow* revealed its protagonist Reginald de Brune at the end of the first volume to be Richard the Lionheart, while *The Unknown* concerned the affair of Bishop Hugh Latimer.

The Romance of the Hebrides, the final novel Lathom published before a long hiatus, was singled out for recognition by MacConochie as the first novel to attempt a depiction of authentic Scottish dialect, and the first novel to attempt for Scottish national fiction what Maria Edgeworth's *The Absentee* had done for the literature of Ireland.[12]

Between 1809 and 1820, the prolific Lathom published nothing. Summers explains that Lathom spent these years travelling and enjoying the companionship of his lover. While this may be true, other tangible clues to what caused Lathom to stop writing and what he did during this period do exist. A deed remains extant at the Norfolk Record Office dated 1809, in which Francis Lathom sold ownership of a house in Norwich's St. George Tombland to his father Henry Lathom and his father-in-law Daniel Ganning (presumably for the benefit of his estranged wife, who, as a married woman, could not legally own property). Judging from the coincidence of this deed being dated the same year Lathom ceased writing for eleven years, it may reasonably be supposed that he received a sufficient sum for the sale of this house to enable him to retire from writing for some years and travel the world.

His next book, *Italian Mysteries* (1820), bears a prefatory letter to the publisher A. K. Newman, dated from New York, October 24, 1819. Because passenger lists were not required to be kept under U.S. federal law until 1820, no record of Lathom's arrival in America exists, but he certainly arrived in the young republic between 1810 and 1819.

Italian Mysteries, while borrowing freely from Lathom's earlier works, was popular enough to be translated into French in 1823, and was apparently well enough received to induce Lathom to continue publishing throughout the rest of the decade.

MacConochie judges from the fact that none of Lathom's works published between 1820 and 1830 were reviewed that the critics must have seen them as inferior to his earlier works and unworthy of review. While it is true that Lathom's Gothic fiction during this period is of a somewhat lower quality than his early work, and that his volumes of short stories, including *Puzzled and Pleased, or The Two Soldiers and Other Tales* (1821) and *The Polish Bandit, or Who is my Bride?* (1824), are of fairly little consequence, some of Lathom's later works are undeservedly forgotten.

The most significant of the novels published between 1820 and 1830 is almost certainly *Live and Learn* (1823), which may be one of the first "gay" novels written in English. In his preface to the novel, which concerns a will bequeathing an old man's fortune to "the first John Brown who shall claim it," Lathom reveals his queer sense of humour when he notes that he is aware of an actual will with a similarly unusual provision. Undoubtedly, he was referring at least in part to his father's singular will. *Live and Learn* features a friendship between two young men, John Brown and the travelling actor David Ferguson, a relationship which Summers described as "clearly uranian." It is true that the best evidence for Summers' contention that Lathom was homosexual probably comes from this novel. In *Live and Learn*, Lathom tells us that the two beautiful twenty year old youths live together alone in a large mansion, spending their time studying Greek and Roman works. Frequent compromising scenes in the novel give further credence to the notion that Lathom was homosexual, or at least included homosexual undercurrents in his work. For example, at one point in the first volume, the manly Brown, carrying his gun, encounters the effeminate Ferguson leaning against a fence, reading Latin poetry. Later, when Ferguson falls dangerously ill, Brown cradles Ferguson's head in his arms, giving him wine to sip and causing him to blush, the implication being that the blushing is owing as much to the intimate nature of the scene as to the effect of the wine. The to-be-expected marriage of Brown with a young woman at the end of the novel does nothing to dispel the sense that there is a much deeper relationship between Brown and Ferguson than meets the eye

The preface to *Live and Learn* gives Lathom's address as "Poet's Alley, Philadelphia"[13] and the preface to *Young John Bull* (1828) is also addressed from Philadelphia. It is accepted that Lathom died suddenly in Scotland in 1832, so he must have returned there at some point between 1828 and 1832. The reason why he would attempt this long and difficult journey in his mid-fifties is unknown. However, Lathom is said to be buried in cemetery ground belonging to Alexander Rennie in the churchyard at Fyvie, Aberdeenshire, Scotland.

As Devendra Varma wrote in his 1968 introduction to the Folio Press edition of *The Midnight Bell,* "*The Inverness Review and Northern Farmer* of Tuesday, 12 March 1901, asked only for a just recognition when it put forward the desirability of erecting some memorial on his hitherto nameless grave."

The Castle of Ollada

The Castle of Ollada (1795) was published when the popularity of Gothic fiction was at its highest pitch; Ann Radcliffe's seminal *The Mysteries of Udolpho* had been issued the previous year, and Lewis's influential *The Monk* saw publication the year following. Lathom's novel, like most Gothic romances written before *The Monk,* owes much of its inspiration to Radcliffe, and—as might be readily seen from the similarity of the two books' titles—to Horace Walpole's *The Castle of Otranto* (1764).

The notion of authorship was conceived of somewhat differently in the late eighteenth century than it is today, and it was extremely common for one author to borrow freely from another. This could range from the frequent custom of outright plagiarism to the less objectionable practice of borrowing character names and certain plot devices. Thus, it is unsurprising to find echoes of Walpole's masterpiece in Lathom's youthful effort in the names of the characters—Matilda, Hypolita and Manfred owe their names directly to *Otranto*—as well as certain aspects of the plot, including the usurping ruler and the prattling servants. However, it would not be fair to dismiss Lathom's novel as a mere plagiarism of *Otranto.* As Allen Grove writes in a preface to another title in this series, *The Cavern of Death* (1794), nearly all Gothic authors borrowed from Walpole to some extent.

The story of *The Castle of Ollada* is primarily that of three young people struggling to bring order and happiness to their disordered and melancholy lives. Altador, like Hamlet, suspects he has been divested of his birthright by his uncle, and still worse, faces some tenebrous obstacle to his marriage with Matilda. Matilda, for her part, indulges a forbidden love for a peasant, Henrico, whilst her father, the Baron Garcia, intends to force her to marry the cruel Gaspero. Henrico is a youth of uncertain parentage whose mysterious situation precludes any hope of seeking Matilda's affection.

Altador is the first in a long line of isolated, even exiled characters, in Lathom's books. In Lathom's next novel, *The Midnight Bell*, young Alphonsus is banished from his paternal estate by his mother's inexplicable injunction, an exile David Punter saw as an example of *Nachträglichkeit*—that is, that Lathom had predicted his own exile from Norwich some years before the fact.[14] Similarly, in *Mystery* (1800), we find Charles Milford leaving his true love and fleeing to Italy, while in *The Fatal Vow* (1807) Richard the Lionheart is obliged to change his name and fly incognito to a distant convent. Likewise, Urbino di Cavetti in *Italian Mysteries* (1820) is forced to quit Venice and seek asylum in the remote countryside. Altador, while not physically isolated like Lathom's later heroes, nonetheless exists somewhere in the margins, shunned by his beloved Matilda and essentially ignored by his uncle, who has deprived him of his birthright and whose castle he inhabits somewhat tentatively.

Gothicized adaptations of the *Hamlet* story were relatively common in the 1790s, and *The Castle of Ollada* in some ways follows this trend. Altador, like Hamlet, is called by supernatural forces to investigate the mystery of his father's death. However, while Hamlet is impelled to action by the ghost of his father, Altador's suspicion is awakened by ghostly lights in his father's now-abandoned Castle of Ollada. In true detective fashion, Altador and his friends resolve to visit the castle and search it for clues. Along the way, his companion Father Anselm informs Altador of his suspicion that the deceased baron was not, in fact, Altador's father: "He never loved you as he would have done, had you been his child." The obviously strained relationship of Altador and his father seems to echo that of Lathom and his father, a relationship that degenerated to the point where his father nearly disinherited him and effectively banished him from his native city. Lathom's commentators, relying on the oft-repeated assertion (a rumour probably spread, for whatever reason, by Lathom himself), that he was the illegitimate son of an English peer, have seen in the youths of unknown birth in his works a reflection of the uncertainty caused by his own illegitimacy. Whether Lathom actually believed Henry Lathom was not his father or whether he invented the idea that he was illegitimate, what is clear is that Lathom, like Altador and Henrico, felt somehow distanced from his father.

The character of Matilda bears a brief mention, as she is an uncharacteristically strong Gothic heroine, especially for a novel penned by a male writer. At one point, she challenges her father's authority, invoking her natural rights as a woman:

> You'll say, because I am a woman; and has a woman then no right to plead in her defence? must she be sold, sacrificed, made traffic of, without the liberty to say she is wronged, or to assert those rights which nature gave to all? I'll call on all the powers of Heaven and earth to vindicate my cause.

Such an impassioned defence of women's rights, occurring as it does only three years after Mary Wollstonecraft's *A Vindication of the Rights of Woman*, is remarkable. Although often characterized as a conservative writer, Lathom in fact frequently displayed liberal sentiments in his works, as with regard to women's rights here, religious tolerance in *Men and Manners,* and the abolition of slavery in *Italian Mysteries.*

The central mysteries of *The Castle of Ollada*, then, concern the explanation of the lights in the abandoned castle and the ghost the simple-minded servants claim to have seen. This explanation will in turn unravel the riddle of Altador's birth, the condition that prevents him from marrying Matilda, and the origin of Henrico.

The pervading atmosphere throughout the novel is one of melancholy, although the melancholy is not yet as pronounced as it would be later in *The Midnight Bell.* The novel, somewhat unusually for a romance of the period, ends if not on a tragic note, at least on a bittersweet one, with the hero Altador failing to win either ownership of the Castle of Ollada or the love of Matilda. The theme of failure to consummate a heterosexual relationship occurs again and again in Lathom's works—in Charles's frustrated love for Marguerite in *Mystery*, in Valeria and Julio's separation in *Italian Mysteries*, and in the case of Averilla and Sylvio in *The Impenetrable Secret*, to name a few—and may have helped fuel the speculation that Lathom was homosexual.

The initial critical reception to *The Castle of Ollada* was generally unflattering. *The Critical Review* exclaimed, "Another haunted castle! Surely the misses themselves must be tired of so many stories of ghosts, and murders,—though to the misses the ghosts of this novel present perhaps the most harmless part of the dramatis personæ." *The Monthly Review* of October, 1795 was less harsh, praising Lathom's description of the tournament scene and his sketches of the characters, particularly the servant Villetta. Interestingly, both critics condemned the novel's morality, one deploring Matilda's decision to elope with a young man she barely knows, and the other decrying the "too favourable a light" in which the group of counterfeiters are portrayed toward the end of the book. The latter criticism is even more strange to the modern reader since Lathom seems to have gone to great length to consecrate his banditti's efforts to the fairly peaceable pursuit of forging coins rather than the rapine and plunder usually resorted to by such ruffians.

Modern criticism of the novel has not been much more favourable. Frederick Frank, in *The First Gothics*, largely dismisses the story as formulaic, and even the usually gushing Montague Summers lavishes but few praises on the book.[15] However, these dismissals of *The Castle of Ollada* are not entirely just. Clearly Lathom did not succeed in composing a novel with the enduring power of *The Castle of Otranto* or the romances of Ann Radcliffe, but such was not his aim. Rather, his aim in writing his first novel was not to indulge his own creative genius, but to adhere to a specific style of romance which would please the general public, in which he was apparently successful. The book is important both in showing the progression of Lathom's art as a writer, and as an example of the type of Gothic novel that was popular during the height of the movement. The novel certainly has its weaknesses. The comic relief of the servants becomes tedious, and the narrative lags in parts. But, on the whole, *The Castle of Ollada* is a solid Gothic romance and contains enough interesting episodes to entertain a modern reader.

Francis Lathom died in 1832, one of the most popular and prolific writers of the day and the author of more than twenty books. He lies buried in a lonely churchyard in the Scottish village of Fyvie, Aberdeenshire, in a grave marked by the wrong name, forgotten, like his works. It is to be hoped that this new edition of *The Castle of Ollada* will begin to stimulate new interest in the life and works of Francis Lathom, and that his novels may finally receive the attention they merit.

James D. Jenkins

Chicago, November 2005

¹ Thanks to Franz J. Potter, who informed me of the existence of the Church of Jesus Christ of Latter Day Saints' Family Search website, where the record of Lathom's christening can be found. These records are also archived on microfiche at the church's Family History Center in Salt Lake City, Utah.
² The will of Henry Lathom, Esq. of Norwich is available for download on the website of the British National Archives.
³ Henry Lathom, Esq., is listed as living in "Catton, near Norwich" in *A List of the Names of Those Members of the United Company of Merchants of England, Trading to the East-Indies* dated April 14, 1789, but the subscribers page of Benjamin Choyce Sowden's *Sermons* (1795) gives the Lathoms' city of residence as Norwich.
⁴ Barringer, Christopher (ed.). *Norwich in the Nineteenth Century.* Norwich: Gliddon Books, 1984, p. 17.
⁵ One contemporary, commenting on Lathom's *Very Strange, But Very True!* (1803), wrote in *Flowers of Literature* for 1803 that, "though not very eminent as a novel writer, Mr. Lathom may be deservedly ranked amongst the modern dramatists, to whom we shall draw the attention of our readers." The reviewer singled out Lathom's final play *The Wife of a Million* for special attention, writing that while the play was "extravagant," it was yet a work of "uncommon spirit and ingenuity."
⁶ Although Lathom's plays were apparently not acted on the London stage, one of them, *Holiday Time, or the Schoolboy's Frolic,* was adapted by Richard Wroughton as *The Dash, or Who But He?* and performed at the Theatre-Royal, Drury Lane in October 1804.
⁷ John Genest, *Some Account of the English Stage* (1832), Vol. V, p. 223, cited by Summers in *The Gothic Quest* (1938), p. 315.
⁸ The marriage record can be found in the genealogical records of the Church of Jesus Christ of Latter-Day Saints, as can the birth records of Lathom's children.
⁹ One of Austen's letters to her sister Cassandra mentions that her father was reading *The Midnight Bell,* which he had got from the library. Presumably Jane read it after he had finished.
¹⁰ The precise date of Lathom's departure from Norwich is quite problematic. Summers alleges that it was in 1802 or 1803, while Devendra Varma, in his preface to the 1968 edition of *The Midnight Bell,* points out that although the *Dictionary of National Biography* gives Lathom's date of departure as 1801, he is listed as a resident at 15, St. Martin-at-Palace Street from 1801-1810. Franz Potter, in a chapter on Lathom in his new book, *The History of Gothic Publishing 1800-1835* (2005), gives Lathom's date of departure (without much explanation) as 1811 or 1812. However, each of these accounts has its problems. It is unclear from Varma's information when exactly the census he cites was taken, and, even if Lathom was indeed listed as the owner of a residence from 1801-10, it does not necessarily follow that, though the owner of record, he inhabited the premises at all times during the decade. In fact, an 1809 deed exists in the Norwich Record Office indicating that Lathom sold ownership to some of his property, including, perhaps, the house where Varma indicated he lived until 1810. I also find that Lathom's

novel *The Romance of the Hebrides; or, Wonders Never Cease!* (1809) provides support for Summers's assertion that Lathom relocated to Scotland circa 1803. *The Romance of the Hebrides* includes detailed information about Scottish customs and an accurate portrayal of Scottish dialect that Lathom likely could not have acquired unless he had resided for some time in Scotland. This, together with the other circumstantial evidence, suggests Lathom's departure was in 1803, as Summers asserted, or at the very least, between 1803 and 1809, not as late as 1811-12, as Potter suggests.

11 The above-cited work by Franz Potter incorrectly states that the will provided two thousand pounds per annum to Francis Lathom. While the will's handwriting is difficult to decipher, it clearly reads "hundred" and not "thousand."

12 Arthur Alastair MacConochie, *Francis Lathom, Forgotten Goth.* Charlottesville, Va.: University of Virginia, 1949 (unpublished thesis), p. 135.

13 I have studied numerous eighteenth and nineteenth century maps and city guides from Philadelphia, but although I have found dozens, if not hundreds, of alleys listed, I have found no trace of a "Poet's Alley" in Philadelphia, either then or now.

14 David Punter and Alan Bissett, "Francis Lathom in the Eighteenth Century", *Gothic Studies,* May 2003, p. 68.

15 This is because Summers probably never actually read the book, despite discussing it at some length in *The Gothic Quest.* He states that the book was published in 1794 with a second edition in 1799, while the true dates were 1795 and 1831, respectively.

NOTE ON THE TEXT

The Castle of Ollada is one of the rarest of all Gothic novels. The Sadleir-Black collection of Gothic fiction at the University of Virginia, one of the most famous such collections in the world, does not hold a copy, nor does the British Library, the Bodleian Library or the Library of Congress. The only copy of the first edition of 1795 I have been able to locate is at the University of Chicago, and to demonstrate how obscure the book is, the library catalogue does not even attribute the work, which was originally published anonymously, to Francis Lathom.

The Valancourt Books edition follows the text of the second edition, published by A.K. Newman & Co. in 1831, a year before Lathom's death. The second edition is as rare as the first, with the only original copy I could locate being housed in the Corvey collection in Germany. The Corvey collection was archived on microfiche, and the sole holding of this microfiche in North America is at the University of Nebraska at Lincoln. The text of this edition is taken from that microfiche copy.

No attempt has been made to modernize or standardize spelling or punctuation, with one exception: Lathom alternates between "Villetta" and "Viletta" as the spelling of the waiting-woman's name; I have changed these all to "Villetta" for clarity's sake. A few other obvious typographical errors have been silently corrected.

Special thanks are due to the staff of the University of Nebraska–Lincoln Libraries' microforms department and to Paul Belloni of the University of Chicago Libraries for their invaluable assistance.

THE

CASTLE of OLLADA.

A ROMANCE.

IN TWO VOLUMES.

"It will have blood, they say; blood will have blood!"

MACBETH.

VOL. I.

LONDON;

PRINTED FOR WILLIAM LANE,

AT THE

𝕸𝖎𝖓𝖊𝖗𝖛𝖆-𝕻𝖗𝖊𝖘𝖘,

LEADENHALL-STREET.

MDCCXCV.

THE

CASTLE OF OLLADA.

A ROMANCE.

By FRANCIS LATHOM,

AUTHOR OF

LIVE AND LEARN; VERY STRANGE BUT VERY TRUE; YOUNG JOHN BULL;
IMPENETRABLE SECRET; ASTONISHMENT; PUZZLED AND PLEASED;
UNKNOWN; MYSTIC EVENTS; FATAL VOW; MIDNIGHT BELL;
FASHIONABLE MYSTERIES; MYSTERIOUS FREEBOOTER;
HUMAN BEINGS; POLISH BANDIT, &c. &c.

" It will have blood; they say, blood will have blood." MACBETH.

IN WO VOLUMES.

VOL. I.

SECOND EDITION.

LONDON:
PRINTED FOR A. K. NEWMAN AND CO.
1831.

The Castle of Ollada

Volume I

CHAPTER I

My heart forebodes some evil.

HOME.

THE sun was just beginning to paint the horizon, when father Anselm (who, according to his daily custom) was sallying out into the woods, near the monastery of Maqueda, heard himself called on, in rather a loud whisper, and on turning round, perceived Hugo, a tenant of the baron of Ollada.

"Oh, I beseech you, father," exclaimed the old man, "come this way with me into the wood: I have a most dreadful tale to relate unto you; come this way, good father, out of the sight of the mansion-house," and thus saying, he turned into the thickest part of the forest, beckoning the surprised father Anselm to follow him, who at length called out, "Stop, stop, old man, we have gone far enough."

"Nay, but come on, I beseech you, good father," said Hugo, slackening his pace; "if my lord the baron, or any one should overhear our talk, I would not, for the world; my neck might pay the penance of my prattling. Oh good father, had you but seen my lord's displeasure, when once I only asked the cause why he had left the Castle of Ollada for this seat, you would know that I had reason for my fears."

"Well, but indeed there is no danger here, so tell thy story; I will watch that no one suddenly break in upon us."

"Beshrew my heart, but I do tremble sorely, father, at the bare thought of what I have seen."

The old man then cast a look round, and continued.—"But I will tell thee speedily, lest we be interrupted. Thou knowest that Friday last my good old mule fell sick and died. Oh! 'twas indeed a loss; he was at once my friend and servant, and loved me as a fellow-creature would have done; nay, by my troth, I think I should not overstep the truth, were I to say he loved me better than men do love each other now-a-days: the times are altered, father—the times are altered."

"Thy fortune, old man," answered father Anselm, "may be changed, as I doubt not but it is; the former baron knew no greater joy than to see those around him blest, and thou wert one, as well as I, who largely shared his generous bounty; but rail not at the times, for, by God's mercy, I trust that there are still good

3

men in plenty to be found, though we may not be blessed in knowing them—but proceed in thy story."

"Well, father, yesterday I hied me to Toledo, to buy another beast, not that I could ever hope it would prove to me what my poor Diego had done: on my return from thence, between—Stay, ay, it was between the hours of nine and ten, I passed the Castle of Ollada; the night was dark and stormy—very dark! I turned my eyes the way the castle stands, though I could scarcely distinguish it: I never come by it but the memory of former days rushes in upon me, and I can't help thinking how happy we should all have been yet, if my good master had not died; ah! father, that word sticks sorely in my throat; dost thou think he died?"

"That he is dead, I have not the smallest doubt," returned the father.

"Ah! father, men may have their thoughts, and St. Jago save us all from the death he died, pray I: and so as I was looking, and looking wistfully at the old turrets, may I never stir my foot from this spot, if I beheld not a glaring light in the very apartment which the baron used to call his study."

"A light! art thou sure of it, Hugo?"

"As sure as that now I am speaking to you, father; and while I gazed upon it, many a time a figure of uncommon size passed and repassed the casement, till, on a sudden, that and the light both sunk into the earth."

"Nay, your imagination carries you too fast."

"No, good father, beshrew me but I do tell you nought but truth; and ever and anon the plumes of him that passed the casement, waved as it were by the violent agitation of his body; oh! the Blessed Virgin defend me from seeing such a sight again!"

"Hast thou mentioned this to any one but me?"

"No, by my troth have I not."

"Then let it not escape thy lips, I charge thee."

"I shall obey thy orders, father; but dost not think it was a ghost, father?"

"A ghost! good Hugo, no, I have no faith in that which never had existence; but leave me, old man; I see young Altador, the baron's nephew, approaching."

"The sweetest youth that ever lived," cried Hugo; "many a time, out of pastime, has he strode my poor Diego." A tear glistened in his eye at the recollection of his mule, he sighed a farewell, and retired among the trees.

4

"That all is not right," said father Anselm to himself, on Hugo's departure, "is, I fear, too true; the baron has of late turned hasty and suspicious, and seemingly is anxious to conceal some secret, which he each moment fears he is betraying; long have I urged him to confide to me the secrets of his heart, and by confession and repentance, seek forgiveness of his sins; but mockery of our sacred rights, and asseverations of his innocence, are all that I could ever draw from him; what this old man hath just related, tallies exactly with my thoughts, but lie they hid."

The holy man advancing a few steps on the way which Altador was coming, thus saluted him—"Health to young Altador."

"Good day unto you, father," returned the youth, "happily met; long have I sought to gain a private audience of you, and chance has now most fortunately thrown you in my way."

"If there be aught, young man, wherein my counsel can assist thy inexperienced judgment, freely ask it, and I will strain the nerve of my abilities to serve thee."

"Tell me then, good father, is it a sin to gratify excited curiosity?"

"What meanest thou, my child?" returned the holy man, with surprise; "explain thyself."

"Swear then, for I have a tale of most mysterious nature to unfold, swear thou wilt be secret."

"By all the saints I will."

"Enough.—Thou must remember that some six weeks past the baron of Ollada, from a wound which he received in hunting, was by his physician pronounced to be on the point of death."

"I do."

"I was then sitting by his bedside, drowned in tears; he looked at me attentively for some time, then having waved his hand, in signal for the attendants and father Benedict to retire, upon our being left alone he seized my hand, raised himself on his pillow, and thus addressed me.

'Altador, I feel the agonies of death approaching fast; I know thy nature to be kind and merciful, and I conjure thee, by thy future prospects of felicity, by that felicity which I have never known, by all thou holdest most dear, shew thy compassion to the greatest wretch that ever felt the bitter pang of keen despair; ease the last moments of my guilty life by thy forgiveness; pardon, oh! pardon, thou injured youth, the ills that I have heaped upon thee; they are thy blessing and my curse. Oh! quick, say thou forgivest me, ere I sink into the dark abyss, that opens wide its fiery jaws, to drag me down to everlasting torture—oh! save me, save me, or I am lost for ever.' He then sunk down in his bed, overcome by the too great exertion of his languid faculties."

"May Heaven grant him that forgiveness which he asked of thee!" cried father Anselm.

"It was some time," continued Altador, "before I could sufficiently collect myself from the astonishment into which his words had thrown me, to answer him, and it was still longer ere he was sensible that I was speaking to him; I expressed my gratitude to him for the care and attention he had shewn me since my father's death, and told him, that far from having any thing to reproach him with, I considered myself as highly indebted to his kindness and liberality; declaring that if he had, by any way unknown to me, injured me, I could not forgive what I had never resented; and finally entreated him to seek forgiveness, where alone he could effectually obtain it."

"What said he to this?" asked the holy man, with impatience.

"He became more calm," returned Altador, "bathed my hand with the tears that followed each other in quick succession down his cheeks, and at length entreated me not to refuse complying with the last request of a dying man: I promised I would do whatever he desired: he then conjured me, immediately on his decease, to visit the antient building, formerly the Castle of Ollada,—" (father Anselm could scarcely conceal his emotion) "and not to leave it till I had visited every apartment, 'for,' said he, 'thou wilt find——' the pangs occasioned by the wound now increasing, he shrieked aloud, and father Benedict entering the room, I retired to my chamber, ruminating on what had passed."

"For Heaven's sake proceed," cried the father.

"I will—Guess my astonishment when a few hours after information was brought me, that his disorder had taken a favourable turn, and that he again wished to see me: I went to his chamber, he called me to him, and again took my hand, saying, that, thanks to the Blessed Virgin, his danger was now over, and he hoped that time and care would work a perfect cure in him: he then said, that he feared he had talked to me in a strange manner, the evening before, but that his fever had run high, and that whilst under its subjection, he had said many foolish and unmeaning things; and with a smile requested me not to think any more of what had passed, and in particular not to give it utterance, as there were always those who were ready to put some dark construction upon the words even of a madman."

"'Tis strange," said father Anselm, "wondrous strange."

"And since his recovery," returned Altador, "many a time has he discoursed with me on his delirium of that night, and has turned all he said into ridicule, but with so bad a grace, that he but ill conceals some fatal secret, labouring in his breast, which he fears to have divulged."

"I fear," returned the holy man, "some deed of horror has stained those walls, and I am much mistaken or you are intimately concerned in it."

"Sure you cannot think my father was——"

"Form no rash conjectures, I beseech you," interrupted the father; "time will bring all things to light, and we must wait with patience till he undraws the obscuring veil that shuts us from the knowledge of futurity."

"Heaven forbid I should accuse any one unjustly," replied the youth, "but your countenance confirmed me in the conjecture I was drawing; if you have any cause for suspicion, tell me, I conjure you tell me."

"I must confess I have often wondered, that your father should have transferred his title and fortunes to your uncle, in preference to you, his only son."

"He could have conceived no dislike against me," interrupted Altador; "I was too young to have offended him when he died; and though I have forgotten his person, I can perfectly remember his telling me one day, as I stood prattling between his knees, and playing with his sword, that I should wear it when I was baron of Ollada, which he made no doubt I should one day be, since my poor brother Ferdinand was dead; he died whilst an infant, did he not, father?"

"I think he was five years of age," answered father Anselm; "he died whilst at nurse with the wife of one of your father's tenants."

Here a short silence ensued, which was broken by Altador.

"And then, father, how very extraordinary that my uncle should suffer the Castle of Ollada to fall to decay, and reside in this small seat; the distance from his own lands can be no object; the castle you know is not above a league distant."

"Have you ever visited it since your father's death?" said father Anselm.

"Never; I have frequently heard the baron declare it to be in so ruinous a state, that it is dangerous to enter it; I did not then think him to be so deceitful as I have since found him; I now see through the cobweb artifice, and nothing, I am determined, shall prevent my exploring this mystery."

"How can that be done?" asked father Anselm.

"Has not my uncle himself pointed out the way to a discovery?" replied Altador.

"You cannot mean to visit the castle!"

"I am resolved on it."

"Be not too rash, I entreat you; your impetuosity and agitation of spirits will betray you, and perhaps close the way to a discovery for ever."

"Promise to assist me when a favourable opportunity offers, and I swear to be guided entirely by you."

"You may rely on me."

"Shall we visit the castle to-day?" said the eager youth; "as the baron has not yet stirred out, we can be in no fear of meeting him, of which we might at any other time be apprehensive."

"You are too impatient, indeed you are, Altador."

"I am on the rack; doubts and fears distract me."

"We are interrupted; I see the hunters going to the chase; come to my cell at eight this evening; I will think on what you have been saying; farewell."

Altador, with great reluctance, and not without repeating his entreaties to visit the castle that evening, was at length obliged to take the path leading to the baron's seat, whilst the holy father bent his steps towards the monastery.

Carefully had father Anselm avoided mentioning to Altador the circumstance of the light appearing in the window of the castle, lest his youthful imagination should immediately have construed the figure into the image of his deceased father, and he should have rushed precipitately to revenge.

Father Anselm could no way account for the light; in spirits he had no faith; he knew that the country was not infested by banditti, who might have made this castle their abode, as a place where they were likely to live undisturbed; the castle certainly was reported by the peasants to be haunted; but then he considered, that as the minds of the vulgar are always prepared to raise phantoms in a mere breath of air, he could not in the least wonder at their having connected an idea of terror with so gloomy and ruinous a building as the Castle of Ollada, the horrors of which were greatly increased by the thick shade of the surrounding forest. Again he thought, that Hugo's imagination might have created this supposed spectre, and his fears have multiplied it into a thousand shapes; might not the moon have shone upon the casements, and produced this appearance? no, that was impossible; the old man had affirmed that it was a very dark night.

Lost in various conjectures, he found himself arrived at the gates of the monastery, where he was met by father Benedict, who told him that the baron had sent a messenger to request their immediate presence; and after father Anselm had taken a hasty repast, the two holy men set out together for the mansion of the baron of Ollada.

CHAPTER II

Be thou blessed—and succeed thy father
In manners as in shape; thy blood and virtue
Contend for empire in thee, and thy goodness
Share with thy birthright.
All's Well that Ends Well.

ALTADOR, not less absorbed in thought than the holy friar, with slow steps reached the seat of the baron, and on entering the apartment, found the lady Hypolita, the baron's cousin, and at this period also, his tender nurse, at breakfast: she was a woman in whom all the good qualities of the heart were united; herself the child of woe, she sympathized in the distresses of others. Early in life she had married, contrary to the will of her father, who dying before a reconciliation could be effected by means of her interceding friends, she was left entirely dependent on her husband: allured by some trifling successes at the gaming table, he had imbibed a most invincible passion for play: fortune, who for a time had smiled favourably upon him, at length withdrew her countenance; and overwhelmed by numerous debts, which he had not the smallest hope of ever being able to cancel, he fell by his own hand, a sad victim to the most destructive of vices.

About this time the baroness of Ollada died in child-birth of Matilda, and the baron wishing to have his only daughter educated under his own eye, had requested the lady Hypolita to un-

9

dertake this charge, of which he knew that no one was more capable; and Hypolita readily accepted the trust imposed upon her.

On Altador's entering the apartment—"This is an unexpected pleasure," exclaimed Hypolita; "I imagined you had joined the hunters, as I have been inquiring for you, and was told you were not to be found."

"The fineness of the morning tempted me to walk in the fields, madam. How fares the baron of Ollada to-day?"

"Thanks to the Blessed Virgin, he has slept well, and is much mended; I am now going to visit him."

"Commend me to him, madam, and say I rejoice to hear of his amendment."

Hypolita moved towards the door, and Altador, unused to dissemble, blushed at the consciousness of the hypocrisy he had been unable to avoid practising.

Hypolita, perceiving his emotion, returned a few steps—"Are you not well, Altador?" asked she.

"Madam," stammered out the apprehensive youth.

"Or do you wish to inquire whether Matilda is so?" returned the lady Hypolita.

Altador blushed still deeper than before.

"Nay, fear not to confess a generous passion to one who is thy friend, sincerely thy friend."

"You know my heart, madam, I see you do; may I then venture to ask, when the lovely maid will return?"

"But one day more will pass ere thou wilt see Matilda; on the day appointed for returning thanks to the All-gracious Powers, who have preserved her father, *she* will return; but I entreat you, Altador, be not too ardent in your love; there is a cause, an obstacle to thy happiness, which I fear cannot easily be removed; would it were not so; depending on thy discretion and secrecy, I will meet thee here to-morrow at this time, when I will give thee some useful cautions, which it is necessary thou shouldst know ere thou seest Matilda: I would say more now, but thy uncle expects me."

Hypolita now left the apartment; Altador could scarcely support himself; he was transported by the idea of again seeing his beloved Matilda, but his heart was rent by the consideration that there was an obstacle to what he deemed the summit of his happiness. That her father had resolved to immure her within the walls of a convent, he could hardly suppose; and, that he had a rival, he found as much difficulty in believing. But in his present state of mind his thoughts could not dwell long on one subject; they now wandered to the discourse he had held with father Anselm, and now to the unconnected words his uncle had uttered—the idea of his fair Matilda wanted its usual charms; gloomy and despondent thoughts weighed down his heart, and the delights of love afforded but small relief to his tortured soul; he was suffering upon the rack of doubt; had his suspicions been confirmed—had he been at liberty to revenge a crime, which was now uncertain, or had he been convinced those suspicions were groundless—but that was impossible; heated as he was by the fire of his imagination, the more he deliberated on the subject, the more strongly was he confirmed in his opinion.

The day was passed by him in the greatest inquietude, every moment was magnified into an hour, and every hour into an endless age, so impatiently did he look forward to the time appointed for his meeting father Anselm.

Towards evening he sallied out from the garden belonging to the baron's mansion, by a gate leading to the monastery: he ascended a small eminence, whence he had frequently, with rapture, admired the glories of the setting sun; this lively scene, painted by the nicest touches of Nature's all-excelling finger, was now unobserved by him, or if by accident he turned his eyes towards it, they seemed to chide the lingering hand of Thetis, for not more eagerly snatching her darling son to her bosom. At length twilight began to expand her dusky wings, and Altador, rising from the bank where he had been seated, set out for the monastery of Maqueda; he passed the northern wall, and entering the western cloisters, soon arrived at the cell of father Anselm, where he perceived the holy man, and Perez, the steward of the baron, who had served the former baron, Altador's father, in the same capacity. The father waved his hand to Altador, to enter, and shut the door; he did so, and the holy man thus addressed him— "You have given me your promise, Altador, to be guided entirely by my advice, during our attempt at this discovery."

"I have," said Altador, "and here faithfully renew it."

"I have determined, Altador, to gratify your curiosity in regard to visiting the castle; God willing, we will enter it this night. Perez will accompany us; the ruins may in many places impede our passage; I am weak, and unable to give you the assistance you may require; Perez is not many years younger than myself, but Nature has bestowed on him a greater share of bodily strength, and he is, I am certain, faithful to our cause."

"Ah, witness all the saints! I were a wretch indeed to be ungrateful to the son of so kind, so good a master," exclaimed Perez, wiping away the tears which the memory of the deceased baron had brought into his eyes.

Altador seized his hand — "I hope," said he, "I shall one day have it in my power to reward thy fidelity, good old man;" then turning to father Anselm, he exclaimed — "Come, father, shall we depart?"

"It is yet too early for our enterprise; we must wait the running of another sand; sit thee down upon this rough-hewn bench, and as I think that thou art but imperfectly acquainted from whom thou art descended, I will relate unto thee such particulars as have met my ear.

"When thy grandfather, Carlos, baron of Ollada, who was descended from the most illustrious race that ever graced the Spanish dominions, had, at the advanced age of threescore and ten, resolved to quit the troops, which he had so often led on to victory, through the routed armies of the infidels, the Spanish soldiers lamented his loss, as the most zealous chieftain that had ever embraced the glorious Christian cause.

"Clad in honours, and crowned with glory, the old baron sought to spend the remainder of his days in domestic happiness, and in the service of that God, in defence of whose name he had so often exposed himself, undaunted, to all the rigours of war, triumphing in the perils which surrounded him.

"Carlos was received in his native country with the most unfeigned joy by all who knew him; they rejoiced in his safety; they gloried in the honours he had acquired; and they triumphed in his victories.

"The Castle of Ollada resounded with merriment and festivity; the gates were open to all; the overflowing bowls and crowded tables bespoke the hospitality of the owner; nor was the feast unqualified by a cheerful welcome to all from the baron himself.

"The baroness, who had been dead some years, had blessed her husband with three children; the eldest was a daughter of great beauty and accomplishments, named Isabella; Ferdinand, thy father, was the second; in him nature produced her masterpiece; how widely different from his brother Garcia, thy uncle!

Ferdinand was generous, noble-hearted, brave, mild, and compassionate; Garcia, subtle, passionate, selfish, arrogant, and cruel; Ferdinand was tall, elegant in his manners, affable to all, and handsome in his person; Garcia, as thou well knowest, not less deformed in body than in mind, haughty to his inferiors in rank, but crouching where he wishes to reap advantage from his feigned humility. They at that period both served in the Christian army, and Isabella was on the point of marriage to don Alvazer, my only brother; but, alas! how precarious is human happiness! The pleasing prospects which the old baron had fondly drawn, of seeing a second generation climb their grandsire's knee, to share his envied caresses, were all blasted by the sudden death of don Alvazer.

"Isabella, regardless of the entreaties of her father, determined to quit the world for ever; and as soon as the necessary preparations could be made for her reception, retired into the convent of Decasca, where she abandoned herself a prey to unrestrained grief; whether she is still living, I have never been able to learn.

"This was a stroke that overwhelmed the unhappy baron with unceasing grief; his passions were strong, and they obtained unbounded dominion over him; his nature, which was before almost exhausted, was unable to sustain the conflict; and his friends and dependants saw themselves in danger of losing him, whom of all men they most revered.

"I now judged it expedient to announce the state of the baron's health to thy father Ferdinand, and requested his immediate presence; but not many hours after I had despatched a messenger to that purpose, the old baron expired within my arms: thy father's tender heart was greatly affected by the recital of the recent and melancholy occurrences; and no where could he look for consolation but in the endearments of his beloved spouse.

"Fatima, thy mother, was a captive of rank, whom chance had thrown into the hands of Ferdinand; her father had fallen in battle by the sword of thy uncle Garcia; such beauty as that of Fatima, which must have warmed the most phlegmatic constitution, could not fail to fire the susceptible breast of Ferdinand.

"Her skin, save where her ruby lips and rosy cheeks opposed a striking contrast to her alabaster bosom, was whiter than the virgin snow of the mountains: her eyes were large, blue, and sparkling, yet mild and conciliating; her height rather exceeded the common size of women, but from the excellent symmetry of her limbs, it appeared rather an advantage than a defect; her mind was enriched with every virtue that could adorn her sex; her heart was the seat of mercy, and if she ever erred, it proceeded from her too great sensibility for the distress of others: from the first moment that she became mistress of the Castle of Ollada, the wretched, whom chance or necessity led thither, never left it unrelieved: her charity was not less famous than her beauty: if perfection ever dwelt on earth, it was under the form of Fatima.

"Ferdinand saw and loved her to distraction; but so great was the delicacy of his honour, that not even the daughter of an enemy, whom the chance of war had made his slave, could he resolve to sacrifice unlawfully to his desires, and custom forbade him to marry her whilst he remained with the army; but no sooner did he receive a summons to return, on account of his father's illness, than he determined to make her his wife; and immediately on his arrival at the castle, announced her baroness of Ollada; and never was there a more faithful convert to the Christian doctrine. The first offspring of their marriage was a son, whom they named Ferdinand; being a child of a sickly constitution, he was entrusted to the care of a peasant's wife, where, as I have before told thee, he died at about five years of age.

"Thou wert born a year after thy brother, on the very day that thy uncle Garcia returned from the army: this was a period that awakened all thy father's fears; Garcia had been struck with Fatima, and had made frequent attempts to tear her from his brother, whilst yet a captive in the Spanish camp; and Ferdinand now foresaw that he had every thing to dread, should the flame be rekindled in the lustful breast of Garcia. But to the inconceivable joy of Ferdinand, Garcia conducted himself with the most becoming respect towards thy mother; and not long after his arrival in Spain, espoused Laura, the granddaughter of the duke of Arvada, who blessed him with the lovely Matilda, of whom she died in child-birth.

"Scarce were her funeral rites performed, ere thy father was seized with a severe illness, which, in less than a fortnight, proved fatal to him. During thy father's indisposition, the subtle Garcia never quitted his brother's chamber, save those moments in which he was attended by father Benedict and father Paul.

"After his death Garcia appeared inconsolable, and shut himself from the world till the interment of thy father had taken place, which he ordered to be solemnized with all possible pomp. Thy father's writings were then produced by him, and amongst the rest, that fatal paper, signed by Ferdinand's own hand, which transfers the castle, title, and estates, all to thy uncle. As every one was well acquainted with thy father's signature, Garcia's right, to what I still believe is truly thine, could not be questioned; and he immediately assumed the title, but never took possession of the castle, saying that he preferred the situation of his own modern seat to the gloomy site of that antique building.

"His next step was to make an offer of his hand to Fatima, which she for a long time peremptorily refused to accept; but at length appointed him to come to the castle on the next day, when she would give her final determination. Garcia arrived earlier than the time appointed, and was met in the hall of the castle by father Paul, who informed him that the lady Fatima was fled to a convent, as an asylum against his persecutions; and that she had refused to inform any one, to what part of the kingdom she was going; 'she has also,' added father Paul, 'left her young son Altador under my protection.'—'He shall be my care,' said Garcia; 'let him be conducted to my mansion.'

"The baron returned home, bursting with rage, and for a length of time, displayed the greatest inquietude of mind, which has gradually worn off; though, as thou canst witness, he is still at times visibly disturbed in mind.

"You were accordingly brought to the baron's mansion, the servants at the castle were discharged, the gates were shut by the baron's own hand, and it has ever since that day continued uninhabited—this is all I know."

"But, oh! father," exclaimed Altador, as the friar concluded his narrative, "tell me, does my dear mother still live?"

"I once heard father Paul say, who was the only person entrusted with the place of her concealment, that kind Heaven had released her from a life of grief; he too is since dead: but think no more, I entreat thee, of that, till we have explored the castle; it is time for us to depart—have you adopted any plan to prevent your being missed by the lady Hypolita?"

"I have," returned Altador; "you need give yourself no concern on that account."

They now left the friar's cell, and passing through a little gate in the southern cloister of the monastery, which opened upon a heath, leading them straight to the forest, inclosed by which stood the Castle of Ollada, at the distance of about a league from the monastery, they set forward with hasty steps.

CHAPTER III

For something there still lies
In Heaven's dark volume, which I read through mists.

DRYDEN.

THE holy man now began to mention the reports that had been circulated relative to the castle's being haunted, but was very careful to treat them with great contempt; and, amongst other things, recounted his conversation with old Hugo, the relation of which, notwithstanding the friar and Perez laughed at it, as the imagination of a weak mind, overcome with fear, had very visible effects on young Altador: a thousand interrogatories did he make concerning it, and seemed displeased with the unsatisfactory answers he received from his companions; nor did the careless manner in which they treated the attending circumstances, lessen his belief of them, but, on the contrary, heightened his eagerness to explore the depths of this mystery.

They were now arrived on the precincts of the forest; the night was dark and cloudy; a few scattered stars served to shew them the towers of the castle, amongst the trees, and they proceeded some paces in silence.

"On which side saw Hugo the light?" asked Altador.

"He imagined on the northern side, in the room which was wont to be your father's study," answered the holy man.

"Many a time have I attended him there," cried Perez; "there it was he said to me, 'Perez,' said he,——"

"Reserve thy story for some fitter time," said father Anselm, interrupting him, "and speak softly, lest any one by chance passing this way should overhear us."

"This is, I think, the western gate," said Altador, pointing to that which faced them.

"Ay, I know it well," cried Perez, who found himself unable to restrain his words; "but if I might advise, let us go round to the northern side; perhaps we shall be able to account for the light which Hugo saw last night."

"Well thought on," said Altador; "I will go immediately."

With hasty steps he turned the angles of the fabric, followed at some distance by his companions: he had now gained the northern side, and retreating a few paces, exclaimed, with a countenance in which were depicted horror and astonishment—"The light, by Heaven!" They all cast their eyes towards the casement in silence; they looked attentively for some time, but could perceive nothing more than a faint glimmering of a purpleish light, reflected on the glass from something within the apartment; they then retreated from the northern side, but not without casting back many a wistful look at the casement. "Some one is confined within this castle," said Altador; "I can already account for the baron's words; let us instantly enter, and restore the unhappy victim to liberty!"

"Stay," said father Anselm; "is it probable that if the baron had imprisoned any one within this castle, he would not have taken precautions against a light appearing through the casement, which plainly indicates that it contains some inhabitant? or that he would even have allowed the consolation of an artificial gleam of light, to one whom, from his confinement, we cannot but suppose to have incurred the baron's highest resentment? Consider that, Altador."

"But is he not well acquainted," returned the youth, "that the castle is reported to be the residence of spirits, and that on this account scarce any one dares approach it after sunset? Let us enter, I beseech you; we are well assured, from my uncle's own words, that no danger can await us."

"I should hope not, Altador; and yet I fear he may have formed some horrid plan to cut thee off, my child; but thou art innocent, and I trust thy good angels will protect thee."

"Will you then venture?" asked Altador, eagerly.

"Strike a light, Perez," said the holy man, "and illumine my lamp."

"I have brought a lanthorn with me," said Perez; "I was fearful the damps might extinguish the uncovered lamp."

"Thou hast done well!" said Anselm.

Altador now drew his sword; the father marked himself with the sign of the cross, and implored the protection of all the saints; and Perez trimmed the wick within his lanthorn. They now ascended the steps leading to the western gate, which moved on its hinges with little reluctance. Altador entered first, followed by the friar, who carried the lanthorn, and Perez by his side, who had uncased his old hanger, long the prisoner of its sheath.

They now found themselves in the great hall of the castle, which was paved with tesselated marble, and by no means in so ruinous a state as they had been led to expect, from the accounts they had frequently heard the baron give of its present condition.

"Ascend that staircase," said father Anselm, "and then turn to the right."

They obeyed the friar's orders, and beheld before them a long and lofty gallery, through which the wind howled in the most dismal strains, and their footsteps re-echoed with hollow sounds: they had not proceeded far, when Altador, stopping short, exclaimed—"Hark!"

"What dost thou hear?" asked the holy man.

"Listen—I conjure you, listen!" said Altador.

They were silent; Perez and the father looked at each other with surprise: after a moment's interval, a deep sigh struck their ears.

"Hear ye that sigh?" said Altador; "our conjectures are now certified beyond a doubt."

"Was it not the wind?" said Perez, casting round a look of apprehension; "listen again." They did, but all was still.

"Would it not be advisable," said father Anselm, "since we are now almost certain some unhappy wretch is here confined, to apprise him, if possible, of our arrival? Will not the sight of us, at midnight, cause great alarm to one, who perhaps, for many years, has been immured within these dreary walls, without beholding one human visage? or if he has beheld one, without a smile to cheer his prison: let us wait till a favourable opportunity offers; we will then come to his release by day."

During this speech they had advanced some steps, and they again heard the sigh much plainer than before.

"Hark again!" cried Altador; "we are sent by Heaven, to the assistance of a fellow-creature, suffering the worst of all earthly tortures; and is not the earliest opportunity the best, to relieve so great an object of pity? Nay, hold me not, for I will find him." So saying, he rushed forward, and having turned the angle of the gallery, after a moment's hesitation, during which the same sound again struck his ear so plainly, as not to leave him the least room to doubt whence it proceeded, he flew, with great violence, against a door on the left: a loud shriek rent the air, and he distinctly heard several voices, as it were in alarm and consultation, but he could distinguish nothing they said.

He now, for the first time, gave way to fear; not for himself, but he trembled lest he should have led his kind protectors, father Anselm and the good Perez, into the power of a banditti: at this idea his blood curdled, every faculty was benumbed, and it was with great difficulty that he supported himself against the wall. As soon as he had somewhat recovered his senses, he listened for the voices he had heard, but all was silent: he now resolved to return to his companions, and communicate to them his cause of alarm, thinking to find them at the turn of the angle, near which he had left them; but what was his astonishment, on lifting up his eyes, to find himself in total darkness! How to account for the departure of his friends he knew not; that they had basely deserted him he could not imagine—that they could have mistaken the way he went was impossible: how was he to proceed in this dilemma? If he called to them, he might by so doing acquaint the banditti where to find him; and such was the nature of the place, that if he proceeded a single step in this thick darkness, he was every moment in danger of falling over the loose ruins that were dispersed along the gallery, or dashing his head against the sharp prominences of the wall, with which this antique building was ornamented. At length he thought he perceived a faint shade of light reflected on the ground, near the other end of the gallery; he resolved, if possible, to come up to it; with much trouble he, after some time, reached the spot, and saw that it proceeded from one of the apartments that opened on the gallery: he entered it, and beheld a chamber which had once been most magnificently fitted up; some of the furniture was still remaining in a very decayed state; the tapestry was torn in many parts, the bed was partly gone, and the remainder lay heaped up in one corner of the apartment, close to which was a door half open; from this the light shone; he entered it, and perceived the lanthorn which Perez had brought to the castle, upon the ground: having taken it up, he instantly cast his eyes round the apartment, in search of him who had carried it, but in vain. The room much resembled the one he had just left, but there was no other door in it, than that by which he had entered. He was now more than ever perplexed to account for the absence of his friends; which way could they have strayed, to have left the lanthorn in the place where he found it? or if they had been carried off by force, how could it have been effected so silently as that he should not have heard any noise? He called on them by name—he re-entered the gallery, and repeated his call, but all to no purpose.

He now determined to return to the apartment where he had heard the voices; those for whose safety alone he was anxious he had lost; all danger now vanished before him, and he knocked at the door as loudly as he before had done: no answer was made: he repeated the knock—all was still silent: he tried to enter the apartment; the door was locked, and resisted his endeavours. "I conjure you," cried he, "in the name of Heaven, I conjure you, whoever you are that inhabit this dreary mansion, refuse not admittance to one, who comes to mitigate a fate he most sincerely pities."

Upon receiving no answer to these words, he resolved to open the door, by making an incision round the lock with his sword; this he with difficulty effected, and perceived an apartment, which in appearance had been lately inhabited; some of the ruined furniture of the castle had been collected in it, and seemed to have been recently in use: through this chamber was a suit of apartments, which ended in a small closet, but there was no single vestige by which he could form the slightest conjecture, how the persons whom he had so distinctly heard could have effected their escape. With sad reflections he returned slowly to the first apartment, and casting his eyes mournfully round, he perceived a mantle of a most beautiful purple hue, suspended before the window; he took it down, and found it to be the garment of a man, which, by the brightness of its colour, he was well assured could not long have been in the situation in which he found it: having carefully folded it, he hid it under his own mantle, and taking up the lanthorn, returned to the gallery. He again called on father Anselm, and on Perez, but without receiving any other answer, save that made by the echo, which seemed to be most strong in the part where he now stood.

Finding that all his endeavours were in vain, and perceiving that the lamp contained within his lanthorn was nearly burnt out, he descended into the great hall; uncertain how to proceed under these circumstances, not less distressing than perplexing, he seated himself on a rough stone, to deliberate what steps were best to be taken: if he returned to the baron's mansion, how was he to account for the absence of the friar and Perez? Again he considered that he might safely go back, for since no one had known of his going out with them, it was very improbable that any inquiry concerning them should be made of him; but then to leave his best friends—those who had visited this ill-reported castle, for no other motive than a wish to benefit him, in so miserable a situation; for their having fallen prey to a merciless banditti, was the only idea that he suffered to enter his mind; the thought was torture, and the reflection that he had no means of rescuing them without betraying all his conjectures to the baron, which he had sworn never to do, maddened him; at all events, he considered it best to return to the baron's seat, lest his absence should raise suspicions relative to where he had been. He accordingly rose, and opening the heavy portal, cast a look of sorrow round, and descended the steps.

It now occurred to him, that if he walked round the castle, he might perchance discover in what part his friends were secreted; he did so, but this search proved as fruitless as the former ones had been: he now hastened towards the mansion of his uncle, and having entered by a small gate, of which he usually kept the key, he repaired to his chamber, and having secured the door, threw himself upon his sleepless bed.

Harassed by a variety of distracting thoughts, the sun had risen ere he fell into a restless slumber, and his repose was then broken by a multitude of unpleasant dreams, not less horrid to the imagination than the real miseries he had that day experienced.

CHAPTER IV

A shepherd now along the plain he roves,
And with his jolly pipe delights the groves;
The neighbouring swains around the stranger throng,
Nor to admire or emulate his song:
While with soft sorrow he renews his lays,
Nor heedful of their envy, or their praise.
But soon as ———'s eyes adorn the plain,
His notes he raises to a nobler strain,
With dutiful respect, and studious fear,
Lest any careless sound offend her ear.

PRIOR.

ALTADOR rose and descended into the breakfast-parlour, against the hour he had appointed to meet the lady Hypolita, resolving to seek a favourable opportunity for informing father Benedict of what had happened, and imploring his advice and assistance.

On entering the apartment, he perceived that the lady Hypolita was not yet come down; and during the interval, he tried every means to raise his sinking spirits, hoping that by so doing, his dejectedness might escape her observation.

In a few minutes she joined him, and after the usual salutations of the morning, and an injunction to secrecy on the part of Hypolita, which Altador faithfully promised to observe, she thus began.

"You must, I think, already have heard, that during the civil wars which distracted Spain in the youth of your grandfather Carlos, none more strenuously supported his king than your gallant ancestor.

Remirez, then duke of Gonsalez, whose extensive domains lie not many leagues distant from the Castle of Ollada, had put himself at the head of the rebels. He possessed great wealth and numerous vassals, but his heart was a stranger to humanity; and as his power gave him great opportunities of exercising his cruelties on those who were so unhappy as to be under his command, he lived amidst his dependants feared and hated; nothing could exceed the malice he harboured against those who embraced opposite principles to his own: oft had he attempted to seduce Carlos from his loyalty, but his fidelity was not to be shaken; thrice did thy grandfather take the haughty Remirez prisoner, and twice were the weighty sums, the price of his ransom, poured into the coffers of thy victorious ancestor.

During his third captivity, the duke died in prison; hence sprung an implacable resentment in the breasts of the descendants of Remirez, against the house of Ollada; and when peace was again restored, and our gracious sovereign had pronounced a general pardon, even then did the revengeful soul of Gaspero, only son of the deceased duke, plan the surprisal of thy grandfather's castle, and the utter extermination of his race, whilst the baron Carlos was in arms against the infidels; but overawed by the certain knowledge that his own destruction must inevitably follow, as the house of Ollada was under the immediate protection of the king, he desisted from his villainous design.

Gaspero was from a child, bold, haughty, commanding, subtle, and impetuous, the slave of passions which knew no satiety, and which were impatient of control; in his person he was tall, active, strong, and hardy; manly beauty shone conspicuous in his face, and shaded the deformities of his heart, from those who were but imperfectly acquainted with him.

The fame of Matilda's dazzling charms had reached his ears, and he burnt with the desire of possessing them: to inform himself whether report had spoken truth, he one day assumed the garb of a pilgrim returning from the Holy Land, and stopped without the gate of this mansion, and in a tale well calculated to melt a compassionate heart, asked alms of the lady Matilda, whom he said he had heard much famed for her generosity.

Matilda, whose artless heart was ever open to the voice of distress, relieved his pretended wants with the most unbounded charity, and the rapturous kiss which the feigned mendicant imprinted on the hand which she extended with her generous bounty, drew the tear of sympathy from her beguiled eye.

He hastened to his own castle in an agony of despair; the concealed flame which he had long nourished, now burst forth, and he resolved to possess Matilda, or die in the attempt. The thought of wedding his race's foe was a stab to his pride; and the impossibility of any other way gratifying his desires, drove him to distraction. He at length determined to send a messenger to this purport, to thy uncle Garcia.—"Gaspero, duke of Gonsalez, grieveth at the animosities that have so long subsisted between his house and that of Ollada: fame hath made him acquainted with the virtues of the descendants from Carlos, baron of Ollada—

23

permit him to know them, and to profit by their good example: let the detestable feuds that now separate their houses cease, unless Garcia will carry his resentment beyond the grave, and revenge the failings of the father on the repentant son."

The unsuspecting baron, not less delighted by the submission of his foe than by the praises lavished on his own good qualities, instantly returned the following cordial answer.—"Garcia, baron of Ollada, harbours no resentment against the dead, nor hatred against their descendants; the feast of friendship shall be spread for the reception of the duke of Gonsalez; let him on the morrow come and partake thereof."

This return to his message, which surpassed his most sanguine expectations, was, to the heated imagination of Gaspero, a presage of future success. The time for his arrival at length came, and Garcia received the duke with unfeigned joy; the tables were spread in the hall of the castle, and loaded with a sumptuous entertainment. Matilda presided; Gaspero's eyes were rivetted on hers, and the blushes which covered the cheeks of the conscious virgin, when she by chance encountered his rapturous glances, heightened, if possible, her all-powerful charms, and added fresh fuel to the flame which preyed upon the heart of her entranced admirer.

Matilda and I at length retired from the banquet; the festive bowls then went round, and the lofty hall echoed with the songs of the warriors. Matilda being gone, Gaspero now studied to wedge himself into the good opinions of her father, and smothering the violent emotions to which his passion had given birth, he succeeded so far as to impress the baron, whom thou well knowest it is no easy matter to deceive, with the most favourable sentiments concerning him.

Matilda petitioned me to walk with her to a little wood, at the distance of about half a league from the mansion of her father: I complied with her request, and we immediately set out: her head was crowned with a wreath of jasmine, her auburn locks flowed in ringlets on her panting bosom, which vied with the lily in whiteness, and shaded it from the heat of the sun; her thin and loose robe displayed the symmetry of her limbs; her cheeks glowed with health, and her eyes blazed with unusual lustre; what an unrivalled prize to tempt the hand of the licentious spoiler!

Matilda (for the heart of innocence and security is always cheerful) sung aloud; she seated herself on a bank, and contemplated the beautiful scenery around her; the sun was verging towards the horizon, and gilded the extreme branches of the trees with the most lively colours; and the small rivulet which ran near her feet, murmured in concert with the pleasing song of the nightingale. On this spot we had continued seated for some time, when the sweetest sounds I ever heard attracted our notice; we turned round and observed two peasants attentively looking at us, through the opening of a bush; Matilda instantly rose, and the peasants having made her a respectful obeisance, retired into the wood; the younger of the two had a pipe in his hand; from this the music had proceeded, which so much delighted us; and as they retired he cast back many wistful looks at Matilda.

Matilda then asked me whether I knew those peasants: I answered her, that I did not, and believed them to be strangers, as I did not recollect having seen their faces amongst those who were wont to pay homage to her father. "Strangers," returned she; "perhaps then they have lost their way, or are in distress, and those sweet sounds might be raised to attract our notice; would we had offered them our assistance!"—"They would have asked it, my love, had they stood in need thereof," I replied.—"Their modesty, I fear, overawed them," said Matilda; "didst not observe how mild their looks, especially of the younger? I feel myself strangely interested in his welfare: his face belies him, or he has a noble mind; 'tis pity that he is not of gentle birth; but, ah! no," continued she, sighing, "he is, I doubt not, happier, in the undisturbed society of some contented fair, than those who wed in palaces."

With these and the like reflections on the part of Matilda, all tending to prove her admiration of the unknown youth, we returned to the baron's mansion.

The duke had departed, but not without exacting a promise from thy uncle to return his visit the next day. However this might be repugnant to his wishes, as he could not, with any propriety, request Matilda to accompany her father, he was obliged to sacrifice one day to the entertaining of the baron, that, from the civilities he shewed him, he might have some plea for the frequency of his visits at the baron's seat.

The next evening Matilda was extremely anxious to revisit the wood, and I indulged her in her wish. She returned to the spot where we had first seen the peasants; she talked of nothing but the enchanting strains of the pipe on which the younger had played, and was unwilling to return, though we had extended our walk much farther than usual.

Many a time did we return to the wood, but to the great disappointment of Matilda, we never met with the peasants; and I now began to think that they really were inhabitants of the neighbouring village, who never having been accustomed to see persons above their own rank, had gazed at us with surprise and respect.

The duke's visits at thy uncle's mansion were now become almost daily, and he contrived never to depart without seeing his adored Matilda, whose presence he was every time more and more loth to quit: frequently did he come hither, unattended, to ask the counsel of the baron on affairs of pretended importance, whose vanity was not a little flattered by the deference which the crafty Gaspero paid to his opinion.

He now determined to declare his love to the baron Garcia, and solicit his daughter's hand in marriage; but there his pride stepped in, and forbade what he considered as a humiliation of his dignity; he now resolved to watch an opportunity of carrying her off by force; but then he considered she might be rescued ere he had effected his design, and thus he might in an instant lose the hope of ever possessing her.

At length, after many severe struggles with his heart, his passion triumphed over pride, and he wrote as follows to thy uncle Garcia—

"Gaspero, duke of Gonsalez, acknowledgeth, with the most grateful remembrance, the favour conferred on him by the baron of Ollada, in again receiving him to his friendship. The duke of Gonsalez revereth the virtues of the man whom he is allowed to call by the noblest title of friend; would he were permitted to call him by the still-dearer title of father. Gaspero hath seen the daughter of the baron of Ollada, and who can see and be insensible to such heavenly graces as adorn the angelic Matilda? they have fired the heart of him who now soliciteth to learn his doom from the illustrious father of the all-excelling damsel, whom Gaspero panteth to name the Duchess of Gonsalez."

The baron was overjoyed on the receipt of this letter, from the consideration that this alliance would greatly add to the dignity of his family; and flew with it to the apartment where I was seated with Matilda: he read her the contents, and then told her, that it was his design that she should immediately receive the duke as her intended husband. Matilda, bursting into tears, fell on her knees, and conjured him, by the love he had professed for her deceased mother, and her, his only child, not to sacrifice her to a man of the well-known cruel disposition of the duke of Gonsalez; urging in particular, the disparity of their years, and declaring her resolution to throw herself upon the protection of the church, rather than submit to become the wife of Gaspero.

The baron, moved not less by our joint entreaties than by his own feelings, which, on cooler deliberation, shewed him the impropriety of connecting his family with a man of Gaspero's principles—for his general character was not unknown to thy uncle, though he saw him with a favourable eye—requested Matilda to compose herself, and to rest assured that he would never compel her to give her hand to any man, on this condition, that she would suffer him to lay the refusal of the duke entirely to her charge. With this proposition she joyfully complied, and the baron Garcia returned an answer in nearly the following words—

"Garcia, baron of Ollada, is highly flattered by the partiality with which the duke of Gonsalez regards his daughter. Garcia knoweth not any one whom he would sooner have chosen as a husband for his daughter, had her approbation ratified her father's choice; but as it is her wish still to continue in an unmarried state, the duke of Gonsalez will forfeit that friendship of the baron of Ollada, which he honours him by so highly valuing, if he urges a suit which can never be granted. On any other terms than the suitor of his daughter Matilda, the gates of the mansion of the baron of Ollada will ever be open to the duke of Gonsalez."

The disappointment of the duke on reading this letter thou mayest easily conceive: to meet with a refusal where he had considered himself as conferring the greatest possible honour on an inferior in rank, was a stroke his pride could ill support; it drove him almost to phrenzy! Policy, however, instructed him to conceal his feelings, and two days after, he ventured again to visit thy uncle: all the subtilty he was master of had been called in, to assist in forming his appearance; his air was dejected; deep melancholy was painted on his countenance; his eyes were fixed on the earth, he spoke but little, and the few sentences he pronounced were unconnected, and broken by frequent sighs. Matilda did not appear: on his departure, after having mounted his horse, he raised his eyes to the window of Matilda's apartment, and uttering a heavy groan, proceeded, seemingly insensible to the repeated farewells given him by the baron, who had attended him to the portal.

It was about a week from this time that thy uncle Garcia received the wound in hunting, which now confines him to his chamber. Gaspero was amongst the first who visited him, and second to none in expressing his concern for the baron's danger, and offering up prayers for his recovery.

It was now my peculiar care to keep a watchful eye over Matilda, whenever the duke came to her father's mansion, as I knew not to what lengths his unbridled desires might lead him, if an advantageous opportunity arose, at a time when her father was unable to afford her his protection.

On the third day your uncle's fever having much increased, and the wound being extremely inflamed, he was pronounced to be in great danger; of this he was himself sensible; and wishing to see you once again, he immediately dispatched a messenger to the monastery of Cordova, where I think you had then been receiving instructions for the space of three years, to request your immediate presence.

On the evening of that day, I prevailed on Matilda, who was ever unwilling to quit her father's chamber, to accompany me to her favourite wood, fearing she might impair her health by too great confinement, to which she was not accustomed.

We had not proceeded far when we were surprised by the appearance of two men, who sprang from a thicket, and planted themselves in the way we were going. "What is your business here?" asked Matilda, in as firm a tone of voice as she could command.

"Our business is with you, lady," answered one of the men; "go with us, and you have nothing to fear; but if you refuse to comply, we must force you."

I now recognised them to be two vassals belonging to the duke, whom I had seen before, and I exclaimed—"Know you who the lady is? the daughter of the baron of Ollada is not to be treated thus with impunity; therefore if you regard your safety, be gone, and tell your licentious master, Gaspero, to beware how he provokes the wrath of one, whose sovereign is his friend."

Matilda, who till I pronounced the hated name, had not entertained the most distant thought of these men being the slaves of the duke, but had mistaken them for robbers, led to this spot by thirst of gain, now seeing herself upon the brink of falling into his power, without the hope of rescue, shrieked aloud, and fainted in my arms.

The ruffians having exchanged a few words together, which I did not understand, one of them advancing, exclaimed—"Threats or entreaties avail not with us, so deliver up the lady, or you may repent your obstinacy."

Matilda, who was just beginning to revive, hearing these words, again shrieked and clung to me closer than before; I now called for assistance as loud as I was able, for one of the villains had seized the trembling arm of Matilda, and the other was endeavouring to wrest me from her; at that instant, a blow from an unseen hand knocked to the earth the ruffian who held the affrighted maid; and at the same time a staff shattered the sword which the man who seized me had just drawn.

"Learn, base slave," cried a voice, "to reverence beauty and virtue; thy life is not worth my taking, but on thy peril presume not to rise from this spot, for that moment is thy last."

Matilda could scarcely believe she was free; she turned to thank her gracious deliverer, and she beheld the young peasant: joy and astonishment deprived her of utterance: his eyes had no longer that pleasing softness, which she had before admired in them; they flushed wild with rage, and bade defiance to the hand uplifted against him; the smiles of peace, which had before possessed his countenance, had now yielded to fury and revenge.— "Fear nothing, lady," said he, "I will protect you, or die in your defence." At this moment two men on horseback burst from the thickest part of the wood, and rode up to their companion, whom the elder peasant had disarmed.

"Who are ye?" asked one of them, "and why have you opposed these men?"

"Because," answered the youngest peasant, brandishing the sword which he had wrested from him with whom he first engaged, and moving towards his friend, who had now three of the ruffians to encounter, "because they insulted helpless innocence, and violated the retirement of beauty."

A shriek from Matilda now caused him suddenly to turn round, and he perceived the ruffian whose life he had just spared, endeavouring to conceal a dagger which he had pointed at the back of his preserver:—"The life I disdained to take before, is now forfeited by thy villany," exclaimed the young peasant; his sword instantaneously followed his words, and the ruffian again sunk to the earth, bathed in purple gore.

Matilda's susceptible nature shrunk from so dreadful a spectacle, and she hid her face in my bosom.

"Thy life shall be the forfeit of the murder thy rash arm hath committed," cried one of the horsemen.

"On equal terms I scorn to shun the combat," replied the younger peasant; "therefore alight."

"The advantage fortune has given me I will use," returned the horseman; and clapping spurs to his horse, drew his sword, and was darting forward on his foe, when the elder peasant advancing, smote the nostrils of the horse with his oaken staff; the beast, stung with the violence of the pain, sprung forward among the trees, and was immediately out of sight.

The two peasants now turned to where the other horseman had stood, but he having conceded half his beast to the disarmed ruffian who had first assailed us, was pursuing the steps of his companion with all possible celerity. The younger peasant now turning to Matilda—"The cowardice of your enemies, lady, has prevented their receiving their deserved punishment," said he.

"Oh, noble, gallant youth," cried Matilda, "how shall I thank thy generous valour? but let us proceed, lest we be again surprised; go with me to my father's mansion; he shall devise some recompence worthy of thee."

"I will accompany thee to the skirts of the wood," answered the youth, "and thence watch thee until thou arrivest in safety at thy father's mansion, but thither I must not go."

"Why," returned Matilda, "will you refuse the honours and rewards that will be lavished on the deliverer of the daughter of the baron of Ollada? my father, valiant himself, esteems the brave; let me entreat you to go and receive the recompence of your courage."

"Far be it from me, lady," answered the young peasant, "to seek any other reward, than that which the remembrance of having preserved your honour from violation will never fail to afford me."

"Alas!" cried Matilda, "thy language and manners but ill agree with thy habit; it is not usual for those of low degree to refuse the offers of their superiors; few there are in thy station, if thy appearance speak thee true, who slight riches and honours: who are ye? for plainly I discern ye are not what ye seem."

"Oh! lady," returned he, "urge me not to a confession that would undo me; my greatest honour is to have deserved thy thanks; they are to me riches and glory."

This conversation brought us to the limits of the wood; the youth then knelt down, and having kissed the hand of Matilda, rose and was retiring a few paces—"Stay," said Matilda; "if you will not accompany me to my father's mansion, take this trifle, as an earnest of my intended services, if you will ever deign to accept them."

She then drew a gold chain from her neck, and presented him with it.—"This, lady," said he, viewing it with the greatest ecstacy, "I will never part from but in death, more worth to me than all the riches of the world beside."

We now proceeded, and the peasants having remained on the precincts of the wood, till we had reached the baron's mansion, immediately retired from our view.

On our return to the mansion, as I considered how much the knowledge of what had happened would hurt the baron, in his present situation, I dispatched a messenger to the monastery of Maqueda, to request the attendance of father Anselm, and father Francisco, resolving to act according to their advice: in a short time they arrived; upon being made acquainted with our alarm, they judged it expedient that some of the baron's vassals should immediately be sent into the wood, in pursuit of the ruffians who had assailed us; I concurred with them in opinion, and ten armed men immediately went out. In about three hours they returned, and informed us, that they had found a spot of ground covered with blood, which they supposed to be that we had mentioned; that the dead body was removed, and that they had traced the track of those who had carried it, for some considerable way, by the drops of blood with which the grass was stained, but at length lost it in the midst of some brambles, through which it appeared they had passed; and that their search of the ruffians who had escaped the peasants' vengeance, had proved fruitless.

On the morrow, father Anselm and father Francisco returned to thy uncle's mansion, and finding his fever much abated, expressed a wish to inform him of the duke's treachery, and consult him on what method was best to be taken for his daughter's future safety.

After some deliberation, it was agreed that I should be his informer. I accordingly entered his chamber, and having at length disclosed the purport of my visit, I was rejoiced to see him bear it with much greater composure than I could have expected: he desired me to tell Matilda, that until he was perfectly recovered, and himself able to protect her, he should send her to the castle of her aunt, donna Isabinda, his wife's sister, a widow lady with only one daughter; and order her to make preparations for setting out the next day; and also to request father Francisco to accompany her.

This request the holy man readily complied with, and early the next morning they set out; it is unnecessary for me, I believe, to add, with great regret on the part of Matilda.

On that day you arrived not long after their departure, at the very moment that I was, according to the baron's request, writing in his name to the duke, upbraiding him with his treachery, and warning him to be cautious how he again approached the mansion of the baron of Ollada.

Since your arrival nothing of any importance has occurred; whatever has happened you are as well acquainted with as myself."

CHAPTER V

Neither man nor angel can discern
Hypocrisy, the only evil that walks
Invisible, except to God alone,
By his permissive will, through heav'n and earth;
And oft, though wisdom wake, suspicion sleeps
At wisdom's gate, and to simplicity
Resigns her charge, while goodness thinks no ill
Where no ill seems.
                                            MILTON.

THE lady Hypolita, at the conclusion of her narrative, offered Altador all the consolation that promises of her friendship, and her wishes to serve him, could convey; at the same time assuring him, that she would use her influence with Matilda, to prevail on her to drive the idea of the young peasant from her thoughts.

Altador once more alone, deliberated again how he might make some discovery concerning his friends; the mystery that hung over the castle was entirely forgotten in his anxiety for their safety: on a second consideration, he feared to place any confidence in father Benedict, knowing him to be a man closely allied to the interests of the baron Garcia, and therefore likely to discover to him whatever he learnt from Altador: the lady Hypolita had given him convincing proofs of her friendship, and he accordingly resolved to trust her with all he knew, and solicit her advice.

To put in execution the determination he had just formed, he instantly returned to the apartment which he had quitted but a few minutes before; he found the lady Hypolita still there, but her head was reclined upon her hand, her eyes were bathed in tears, and a deep sigh stole from her bosom. Altador, on entering the apartment, was, for a moment, dumb with surprise; he then approached her, and tenderly inquired the cause of her emotion.—"Forgive me, Altador!" she exclaimed; "I saw you not; my thoughts were in the grave. Blame me not that I paid the tribute of a tear to all I once held most dear. You marvel at my words: may you never have the cause for grief that I have had! I have felt the wrath of a father, alienated from his child; I have seen a husband, driven to desperation, fall the victim of his own hand; and, to complete my curse, my only hope, my darling boy, was snatched from me; yet, the Blessed Virgin is my witness, that I have never uttered one complaint against those who left me, friendless, unprotected, to the griping hand of poverty and affliction; for the decrees of Heaven are just, and mortals must endure their sufferings—not murmur at the all-directing hand of Providence."

A flood of tears now came to her relief, and she became more composed. Altador then asked her to entrust him with her melancholy history, apologizing for this renewal of her sorrows, by the concern he took in her welfare. She readily complied with his petition; and having briefly related the manner by which she had incurred her father's displeasure, and the death of her husband, don Gomez, she proceeded by telling him, that a few months before her husband's death, she lay in of a male child, whom she immediately placed out in the country, with a woman who undertook to nurse him; and that before twelve months were at an end, she, to her inexpressible grief, received intelligence of his having died suddenly in a fit:—"At the moment you entered the apartment," continued she, "I was thinking that had Heaven kindly spared my boy, he might have been a gallant noble youth, as you now are, the pride and comfort of his doating mother; but 'twas Heaven's will that it should not be so, and I must not repine: yet 'tis no sin to bathe his memory with my tears, and feast upon the thought of what he might have proved; but he is blest, and I am resigned." Recollection now became too painful, and leaving the room, she retired to her own apartment, where she gave full vent to her sorrow.

Altador though he feelingly participated in her griefs, could not but lament the loss of an opportunity so very precious to him; and as he knew that on Matilda's return, the lady Hypolita would continually be with her, and thus a considerable length of time might elapse, ere he should be able to obtain the conference he so earnestly desired, he resolved to go immediately to her apartment. But as he was passing through the hall, his attention was arrested by the sound of a carriage; he moved towards the portal, and perceived the object of his wishes, the lovely Matilda, descending from the vehicle he had just heard.

Not more irresistibly beautiful appeared the goddess of love, when rising from the azure deep, the sea-born nymphs first pressed her coral lips, than did Matilda to the enchanted senses of the gazing Altador: with ecstacies he welcomed her return, and she thanked him with a smile heightened by the tear of joy that glistened in her piercing eye, for she loved him as a brother.

Instantly she flew to the chamber of her father, where she mingled her congratulations on his recovery, with thanks to the all-gracious Powers, who had preserved him to defend her against the man whom she dreaded as the avowed disturber of her peace, the duke of Gonsalez. The baron embraced her with all the transports of parental fondness, nor was he less lavish in his acknowledgments to the father Francisco, the faithful guardian of his beloved Matilda.

Father Francisco was humble, meek, and truly pious: his aspect was calculated to inspire reverence and love; his words, for they proceeded from the heart, sunk deep into the mind, while the purity of his life and manners enforced the precepts he delivered: he had inculcated the sublime truths of the purest religion into the heart of Matilda, and poured the balm of peace and consolation into her bosom, while agonized with distracting fears for her father's recovery.

It was now the lady Hypolita's turn to bestow her caresses on Matilda, the pleasure of which was greatly enhanced to the receiver of them, by her long absence from one whom she tenderly loved; and never did an anxious mother receive a long-lost child with greater transports, than Hypolita expressed on again clasping Matilda to her bosom; nor was there a domestic in the mansion who did not express the most unbounded delight on again beholding *her*, whom they esteemed as their kindest friend; and her faithful dog Luco frisked and bounded before her, striving to convince her of his joy at her return.

The day passed, but no favourable opportunity presented itself to Altador for his intended conversation with the lady Hypolita; towards evening, he, to his great mortification, saw Matilda and Hypolita, attended by two of the baron's vassals, stroll into the fatal wood; he joined them, and the conversation, of course, turned on indifferent subjects. Happily for Altador, they met no one in their walk; this, which was a source of great joy to him, had a very opposite effect on the lady Matilda, who had set out with a countenance dressed in smiles; while Altador's aspect on their first entering the wood, had been overshaded with the deepest gloom.

Night at length arrived, but to the great disappointment of Altador, he could neither venture to the castle, nor to the apartment of the lady Hypolita, as the greatest part of the baron's domestics remained up, during the whole of the night, busied in preparations for the feast, which was to take place on the morrow.

Towards midnight he retired to his restless bed, and after some time fell into a profound sleep: he dreamt that he was in an apartment of the castle, much more desolate and gloomy than any one he had yet seen; that he felt a dread upon him, as it were of some unusual sight which he had been warned he should behold, and which would proceed from one of the numerous doors that opened into this apartment: at length, a human figure, pale and wan, stood before him, he instantly felt a wish to embrace it, and upon his approaching towards the spot where it stood, it presented a bloody dagger at him, and uttered a loud shriek: upon this he awoke; his dream was still clear to his imagination, but he attributed it only to the disturbed state of his mind, and again composed himself to sleep: his dream was not yet ended: he now thought himself in the small closet, terminating the suit of apartments in which he heard the voices, when he visited the castle; he fancied he saw the floor open, and the same figure rise, and beckon him; but by the inconsistency of action natural to dreams, he now avoided it, and retreating backwards, stumbled over a corpse, still warm and bleeding: upon seeing this, he again awoke: the figure he had beheld was strongly impressed upon his recollection, wan and emaciated, but whether male or female, he knew not; he lay considering what all the visions he had seen should portend, when sleep again overcame him, and he once more sunk upon his pillow: his repose was still interrupted; he now thought himself in the long gallery of the castle, attentively viewing a portrait, of which the canvas appeared to be animated; it represented a man in armour, chaining a lady to a pillar of marble, and vehemently threatening her, whilst she seemed in the most piteous strains to implore his mercy; he now drew his sword, and was rushing to her assistance, when he felt himself pulled back by father Anselm, who called to him to forbear, and follow him: he obeyed, and had not proceeded many paces, when he perceived Perez, holding a lamp to light him on his way; he had now followed them round an angle, the walls of which were stained with blood; when he was awakened by a servant knocking at his chamber door, and calling him to attend his uncle, the baron Garcia, at breakfast; he immediately sprang from his bed, and began to dress himself; and as he had no faith in any supernatural revelations, when he became more composed, he smiled at the uneasiness which his dreams had at first occasioned him.

He now descended into the lower apartment, and with as good a grace as his feelings would permit him to assume, congratulated the baron on his recovery, who, on his part, received Altador with great cordiality and affection, as he always was wont to do: as Altador had deferred leaving his chamber to the latest moment, breakfast was just ended as he entered the apartment, and the tolling of the bell a few minutes after to summon the family to the chapel, though it relieved him from the disagreeable situation he was in, under the immediate inspection of the baron's scrutinizing eye, fell like a weight of lead upon his heart, as it warned him, that the moment was fast approaching in which the baron would become acquainted with the absence of father Anselm and Perez; with difficulty did he support himself; but his uncle, who either did not perceive his emotion, or wished to appear unmindful of it, took his hand, saying—"Come, my dear Altador," and they entered the chapel together, followed by the lady Hypolita and the blooming Matilda; here they were met by all the friars of the neighbouring monastery, as also by the baron's dependants, domestics, tenants, and vassals, who had assembled on this joyous occasion. Father Benedict performed

mass; no sooner was the celebration ended, than the baron inquired of father Francisco, who happened to stand nearest to him,
where father Anselm was? but without waiting for an answer, he
turned towards father Benedict, and repeated his inquiry; the holy
man replied—"That no one of the monastery had seen him since
the evening prior to the last, and that they knew not whither he
was gone."

"Did not I on that very day command him to attend here at
this hour? Say, did I not, in thy hearing?" asked the angry Garcia.

"You did, my lord; you sent for us on purpose," said Benedict.

"I plainly see how it is," returned the baron; "I have known
him long; he is one of those that dearly loved the former baron,
my brother; and now this caitiff friar thinks it is a sin ought to
diminish of his prayers for him that is dead, to give unto the living—mark my commands; let him instantly be sought, and him
who ere to-morrow's sun arise shall bring him to my sight, I will
reward; the ill-dissembling hypocrite shall rue his disobedience to
my word."

"Nay, my good lord," interrupted the lady Hypolita, "some
unforeseen accident may have prevented his attendance; I pray
you mitigate your wrath; let not your displeasure mar the general
merriment of this day, I beseech you, good my lord."

"No!" exclaimed Garcia, "I will revel with increased delight; I
now am certified in those suspicions which I long have entertained: has Perez been commanded plenteously to regale my vassals? call him hither."

"Perez has also been missing since the evening before the
last," said one of the domestics.

"'Tis well!" exclaimed the baron, now almost choked with
rage; "let him also be sought; he who discovers him shall not go
unrewarded; follow me, father Benedict."

They instantly retired to the baron's apartment. This was an
hour that the designing Benedict, who, for private reasons, detested father Anselm, had eagerly longed for, and he now determined to turn the favourable opportunity which chance had given
him to the greatest advantage he was able; accordingly he omitted no inuendo that might tend to prove father Anselm's dislike
to the present baron; and thus he more strongly exasperated
Garcia, whose resentment was already excited in no small degree;

37

and concluded by assurances of his own attachment, and willingness to serve the house of Ollada.

The banquet was now prepared in the hall, and the company assembled; Garcia entered, and saluted them with the most seeming respect; he pushed on the feast to a late hour with unrestrained gaiety, and plied his guests with repeated goblets of wine; he also indulged himself with plentiful draughts, but he carefully avoided intoxication. No sooner were the guests departed, than having wished his family a good night, he retired to his chamber, saying, that the pleasures of the day, to which he had for some time been unaccustomed, had much fatigued him.

Altador now stole cautiously to the apartment of Hypolita, and having knocked at the door and found her alone, he entered, and began to inform her of the reason of his late visit.

Matilda, whose thoughts never wandered from the dear possessor of her heart, but they returned to him with increased delight, had stood some time musing at the window of her apartment, and was just beginning to undress, when she was alarmed by a quick rapping at the door, accompanied by these words— "My lady! my lady! lady Matilda! open the door, I beseech you, my lady!" Matilda finding it to be a female voice, complied with the request; and upon her opening the door, in rushed her waiting-maid Villetta, who flinging herself into a chair, exclaimed— "Oh, my lady, I am sure it will break my heart to leave you, but I can't stay here, I can't indeed!"

"For Heaven's sake," cried Matilda, in the greatest astonishment, "what is the matter? What do you mean?"

"Oh! my lady, I have seen it again; my heart was in my throat, and I trembled—Oh! holy Maria, protect us, how I trembled!"

"Seen what?" asked Matilda.

"The ghost! my lady, the ghost!"

"The ghost!" repeated Matilda, still more confounded than before.

"Ay, my lady, I never told you of it before, but I must tell you now."

"Well, begin then, and let me hear what it is that has so much alarmed you."

"Perhaps you never saw a ghost, my lady?"

"No, nor you either, I believe; but let me hear what it is you have seen."

"Yes, my lady, I am going to tell you: why you must know, my lady, that last winter, Jerome, the old butler—hark! is not that somebody coming up the stairs, my lady? pray listen!"

"No, no, it is only the wind; why, you do not imagine there are any ghosts here, I hope?"

"Nay, my lady, God knows best; but as Jerome says, I warrant now they have got so close to the outside of the house, they will soon get in; but, however, that is none of my business; I shall be far enough off by that time; it will be bad enough for them that stay, I am certain."

"Why don't you tell me what I asked you?" cried Matilda.

"Well, my lady, so last——either December or January, I can't rightly tell which, but one of the two it was however—stay, my lady, when was it that your dog, Luco, was lost? for it was the day after, I well remember."

"In January, I believe; but what can the exact time signify?"

"Ay, my lady, so it was January—poor beast, how he did fondle about me when he came home, and jumped and frisked! but that has nothing to do with what I was saying; and so, my lady, one night about that time, says Jerome to Lopez, says he—I forgot to tell you, my lady, that Jerome's sister, that lives at the bottom of the hill, was very ill, and dying as every body thought at that time; she is wonderfully mended for a woman of her age; don't you think so, my lady?"

"Yes, yes," said Matilda; "but go on."

"Well, my lady, when all the family was in bed, he asked Lopez if he would sit up an hour or two for him, whilst he just walked as far as his sister's and back again; it is not very far, you know, my lady; so Lopez said he would; for he is a very sweet-tempered young man, as any in Spain, and willing to do any body a kindness; so he let out Jerome and locked the door: so when he was gone, I says to Lopez—Lord, my lady, an't my face bleeding? I am sure I hit it a terrible knock just now, as I was coming up stairs; the ghost put me all over in such a twitter, I did not know where I went, nor whether I stood on my head or my feet, I am sure: don't it bleed, pray, my lady?"

"No," answered Matilda, "the skin is not cracked."

"Well, I am sure it felt as sore as if it had. So, my lady, I says to Lopez, 'Lopez,' says I, 'as you are alone, I won't leave you by yourself at this time of night; I'll keep you company till Jerome comes back, shall I, Lopez?' we were always rather particular to one another, my lady; and so you know, my lady, I thought he would be very proud of the offer; but instead of that, as it happened, my lady, he said, says he, 'I would rather you would go to bed, Letty,' he always calls me Letty, so does my lord, the baron, sometimes; 'for I am sleepy,' says he, 'and I shall doze till Jerome comes home, so I can't talk to you.'—'Well,' says I, 'Lopez, you need not talk, nor do any thing else, without you like it, but I'll sit and work by you, I am determined;' I was making myself a new veil out of one of your old ones, my lady; don't you remember the black spotted gauze one, madam, that you used to wear?"

"Not exactly," replied Matilda, who began to grow weary of her prating; "but pray go on with your story."

"Well, madam, so I kept sitting, and Lopez kept nodding, so at last I really saw he was tired; but he often begged of me not to sit up after my time, as I should be weary the next day, and teased me very much to go to bed; but I would not, because I had said I would not, and I did not choose it; so when we had been sitting about two hours, or it might be two hours and a half——"

"In what part of the mansion were you?" asked Matilda.

"In the little room by the side of the portal, my lady; it is a comfortable little place; I wish I may have just such a one when I am married to Lopez; so my lady, as I was saying, while we were sitting, there came a rap at the window, just so, my lady; 'there is Jerome,' says I.—'Well,' says Lopez, 'go you to bed then, and I will let him in;' and he gave me such a smack.—'No,' says I, 'I will stay and shew him that I sat up for him too; besides, I want to hear how the poor woman does.' You know it was very natural, my lady, when the poor creature was so ill; I always pity sick people from my heart, I do.—'Well,' says he, 'I won't open the door while you are here, so you may as well go; what do you suppose folks will say of us, sitting up here, all alone, at this time of night?'—'Well,' said I, 'I am sure I have been doing nothing that I am ashamed of, and so I can face any body:' there was another rap at the window, just then, my lady, 'and I'll open the door myself,' says I; and then there came another rap: now you know, my lady, a ghost always knocks three times.—'No,' says Lopez, says he, upon that, 'I'll open it then;' so he opened the door, my lady, and shut it again directly, and I thought he looked very queerly, and he said—'Oh,' says he, 'there is nobody at all; it was only the wind,' and he walked up to the fire-place, my lady, and sat down. Well, my lady, I could not but help thinking but he had seen something that had frightened him, and that he durst not tell me, for fear I should be frightened too; so I brushed past him and popped my head out of the door, and, holy Maria defend us! there I saw a tall, tall ghost, all in white, stalking up the lawn; and when I opened the door, it turned about and looked at me, and I was so terrified, that I flopped down in a fit, in less than a moment. Oh! my dear lady, you cannot think how frightful it is to see a ghost!"

"Well, and is that what has so dreadfully alarmed you now?" said Matilda.

"Oh, no, my lady, a great deal worse; but I have not done my first story yet: so when I came to myself again, there was Lopez had been pouring a heap of water all over me, and made me quite wet; and there was Jerome come back, and he had seen it too, my lady, and the poor old man trembled like I don't know what, my lady; and Lopez he laughed at us, and said, we did not know what we saw, but I told him that two peoples eyesight was better than one, and that he should not persuade me out of it.

"Well, my lady, but then about to-night; ay, my lady, the ghost at the castle, for they say it lives at the castle—oh! blessed Virgin, my lady, what a terrible story Jerome once told me about that castle!—'Villetta,' said he——"

"Let me hear the conclusion of this story first," said Matilda, "and then perhaps I may attend to the other."

"Ay, my lady, I am sure you will like the other best, for it clears up, as it were, all about who the ghost is: well, my lady, and so the ghost of the castle did not like all this feasting that was going forward here to-day; that was the reason of his walking to-night, Jerome says, and he is reckoned a very sensible man in those kind of things, my lady, and they say he understands spirits as well as any body: well, my lady, so to-night there was I, and Flora, and Lopez, and Jerome, and Pedro; the rest of the servants were gone to bed, and we were sitting and hearing an old story of Jerome's; he can tell a terrible story vastly well, my lady; and so in the middle of it, says Flora, says she, 'It rains,' says she; 'the Holy Virgin defend us from a tempest!'—'Tempest!' says Pedro, 'the day has not been hot enough; besides, the sky does not look like one.'—'Sky!' says Lopez; 'how can you see that when the shutter is shut?'—'Well,' says Pedro, 'I'll open it, and shew you.'

"So we saw it was very dark and rained, but Pedro was right enough, for it did not look like a tempest; so they sat down again, and Jerome went on with his story; so presently Flora gave such a shriek.—'There,' says Lopez, 'you are quite out, Pedro, it lightens.' Well, my lady, I am vastly afraid of lightning myself, but I could not help turning to the window, for all that, and I called out, 'Oh! Heaven defend us all!' says I, 'there is the great tall white ghost again!' so Pedro snatched up a candle, and ran away to bed, and so did Flora, and Jerome fell upon his knees and began to pray, and Lopez ran to the window, and, 'Ghost,' says he, 'why it is only the cream-coloured mule!'—'Well,' says I, for I was in such a passion with him, for pretending to be so courageous, 'well,' says I, 'I wish you was upon his back—that is all the harm I wish you,' and directly I ran away to you, my lady, for I dare not sleep in my own bed—I dare not indeed, my lady."

"For shame, Villetta," cried Matilda, "how can you suffer such childish fears to get the better of your reason? You see Lopez was not alarmed by any such nonsense; and I make no doubt but the conjecture he formed concerning this supposed ghost was a very just one."

"Ay, my lady, I am sure Lopez was as much afraid as any one of us, only he wanted to shew his courage; but indeed it was a spirit, my lady; Jerome knows all about it; and I would not sleep again in my own chamber——"

"But why should you suppose yourself safer in my room than your own?" asked Matilda.

"Because you know, my lady," replied Villetta, "my chamber is directly over the portal, and that is where the ghost first appeared, you know, my lady; and if you knew the story about who the spirit is, my lady, I dare say you would be terrified to death."

"You seem very desirous to relate it," cried Matilda; "so as I am somewhat weary, let us go to bed: put out the lamp, and then you may tell me what else you have heard concerning this dreadful spectre."

"Then I may stay here, my lady, may I? all night, my lady, pray?"

"Yes, yes," cried Matilda, "but on the morrow I shall certainly inform my father of this dreadful alarm, and desire him to lay this terrible spirit."

"Oh, my lady, Jerome will tell him, ere you are stirring; he swears he would not stay another night in this mansion, for all the baron is worth; but pray, my lady, do not tell him what I am going to tell you now; pray don't, my good lady."

"I make no conditions," answered Matilda, "come, get into bed, and extinguish the lamp."

"Lord, my lady," exclaimed Villetta, "what! tell a story about a ghost without a light in the room! I would not for the world; I dare not indeed, my lady."

"Well then, let it burn," said Matilda, "but set it on the hearth, lest it be productive of any mischief."

"Oh, holy Maria!" exclaimed Villetta, as she was stepping into bed, "a sad thought is just come into my head."

"What is it?" asked Matilda.

"Nay, my lady, I do not pretend to know any more than other people, and perhaps not quite so much as some do; but I would wager my life the ghost has got poor Perez and father Anselm into his wicked clutches; for you know, my lady, they have been missing some time: he'll make confession of his sins to the father, or tell him some murder that has been committed, or something I make no doubt, and so we shall hear all when he comes back."

Matilda could not help laughing loudly at this extravagant idea of Villetta's, who immediately exclaimed—"Ay, my dear lady, you don't think so, because you have not seen the ghost, and pray the Virgin you never may: but had you even heard what Jerome told me—'Villetta,' said he, 'I tell *you*, because you are discreet, and won't blab.'—'No, no, Jerome,' says I; 'you may depend on me, I won't.'

"Then I insist on not hearing it," cried Matilda; "if he told it to you in confidence, my curiosity shall not be gratified at the expence of your faith."

"What then you won't hear it, my lady?"

"Certainly not," answered Matilda; "remember the condition on which Jerome entrusted you with this secret, on which you seem to set so high a value."

"Why to be sure, my lady, I did promise him I would not say any thing about it, for fear of getting him my lord's ill will; but I thought just to you——"

"In this case I am no more than another," answered Matilda, "and your having broken your promise in order to relate a secret to me, in preference to any other, is no palliation of your offence; compose yourself and go to sleep—good night."

"Good night, my lady. Are you sure you locked the door, my lady?"

"Certain," answered Matilda, "so once more good night."

"Good night, my lady."

Matilda was nearly asleep, when Villetta, pulling her by the arm, cried—"Madam, my lady, did you think to look under the bed, my lady? I am sure I heard a noise."

"What is the matter now?" said Matilda, half asleep.

"I heard a noise, my lady," said Villetta; "Oh, Lord! there it is again! there is something under the bed."

Matilda raised herself on her pillow and listened attentively, while Villetta clung to her, as if that moment had been her last; Matilda plainly heard, as it were, some one breathing very loudly under the bed; she determined to see what it was, and jumping out of bed, took up the lamp for that purpose, while Villetta hid herself under the bed-clothes; Matilda raised the valance, and perceived in a sound sleep her dog Luco, who had followed Villetta up stairs, entered the apartment, and crept under the bed unperceived, whilst Matilda's attention was fixed on the alarmed Villetta.

Villetta now ventured to breathe again; fear had for some time suspended her respiration, and Matilda, having turned Luco out of the room, and re-entered the bed, they at length both fell into a profound sleep.

Altador had in the mean time found great alleviation of his sorrows, by relating them to one who took so feeling a part in them as the lady Hypolita; she heard his narrative with surprise and pity; she wished to counsel him for the best, but she knew not what advice to offer him; for no sooner did she form in her mind any plan that wore a favourable appearance for sounding the depth of the mystery in which the castle was involved, than some obstacle arose, which rendered it impracticable; and she finally determined not to fix on any thing till after a night's deliberation.

The lady Hypolita had appointed Altador to meet her after breakfast in the garden: morning was now come, and as he was descending into the hall, he heard a great confusion of voices, and the baron's amongst the number; when he approached near enough to distinguish what was said, Lopez uttered these words—"An't you ashamed of yourselves, you blockheads you, to disturb the baron about your idle fancies?"

"Indeed, my lord, it is true," answered Pedro; "there were Flora, and Jerome, and Villetta, and I, we were all——"

"Ay, sir," cried Jerome, "and the first time I was all alone by myself."

"Yes, but I saw it, as well as you," exclaimed Villetta, who now rushed past Altador on the stairs.

"Yes, and I saw it last night," cried Flora, "as plain as I now see you, Lopez."

"Hold your tongue, Flora," said Lopez, "and don't tell the baron lies."

"Lies!" exclaimed Flora, "lies! I scorn your words—you would not have said so to Villetta."

"And pray what business is that of yours?" cried Villetta, bouncing up to her; "now, my good lord, let me tell the story," continued she, turning to the baron Garcia.

"Silence, I command you all," exclaimed the baron, "and hear me; silence I say."

"Silence, silence," echoed Lopez; "did I not tell you not to make so much noise? Silence."

"Speak one of you at a time," continued the baron; "I ask what you have seen?"

"Speak, Jerome," cried Pedro.

"No, the baron spoke to you," returned Jerome, "do you speak."

"Why don't you answer, Pedro? what was it you saw?" repeated the baron.

"Please you, my lord, I saw nothing; I only heard Flora or Villetta, I don't know which, say that——"

"Oh! it was I," exclaimed both the females at once, "it was I."

"Well, sir, they said—says Villetta, says she——"

"No, it was I spoke first," interrupted Flora.

"This trifling is intolerable," cried the baron; "do you speak directly, Jerome."

"Yes, I saw the ghost twice, and my old limbs shook again with fear, I can truly affirm; and unless your lordship gets it laid, I must quit the mansion, though I am very old, and Heaven knows how I shall be able to live, but I must leave your lordship unless it be laid."

"And so must I," exclaimed every servant present, except Lopez and two others.

"Should you know this spirit again, were you to see it?" asked the baron.

"Oh yes, my lord!" exclaimed Jerome, Pedro, Villetta, and Flora.

45

"Why, you did not see it, Pedro?" said Villetta.

"Yes," answered he, "yes, I had just a glimpse of it; a frightful black squabby thing with two great eyes; Saint Jago preserve us, how it did stare!"

"Black, you fool!" cried Villetta, "it was as white as my petticoat, and as tall, a great deal taller, than any man."

"Grant me patience!" exclaimed the baron, "are you all mad? are you raving? You, Jerome, I suppose, affirm that it was blue; and you, Flora, that it was red."

"Oh! no, my lord, white, white," they both answered immediately.

"And do you really think you should know it again?"

"Quite certain, my lord," they all replied.

"And have you no idea whence it came, or whither it went?"

"Why, yes my lord," cried Pedro, "Jerome says——"

"Oh! I said nothing," interrupted Jerome, "only that I thought it was very likely it might have taken up its abode at the castle, as being an old ruined place, where nobody would go to disturb it."

"Yes, my lord, all the neighbourhood says the castle is haunted; nobody dares go there," added Villetta.

"'Tis well," said the baron; "then do you all meet me here an hour hence, and we will proceed to the castle in search of it;—no murmuring; those who do not instantly and readily comply, shall repent their disobedience." So saying he left the hall, and entered the breakfast apartment.

Altador, who was all astonishment at what he had heard, now called Jerome aside, and asked what was the cause of this alarm?

"Why, my good master," answered Jerome, we conjecture——"

"What then," cried Altador, "was all this confusion raised merely from a simple conjecture?"

"No, no," returned Jerome, "we are sure enough that there is a spirit that is eager to get into this mansion, but whether a good one or an evil one, so bless me Heaven, I cannot tell; but we can only conjecture who it is, that was what I meant, but that there is one, we are certain; why, my good master, I saw it last night, and so did Villetta, and Flora, and Pedro, ay, and Lopez also; but it is not to his interest to say so; a man must not let his words cut his throat, be he ever so terrified; Lopez knows secrets, I am well assured, but that is none of my business."

"But," asked Altador, "may I not know your conjectures concerning it?"

"My lord the baron must not know then for the world," cried Jerome.

"Depend on me he never shall," answered the youth.

"Why, my good master," said Jerome, "I have often thought that there have been black doings in that castle, or why should it be shut up as it is? But I said nothing, for it was none of my business; but some of the servants—is not that somebody coming along the passage?"

"I believe not," answered Altador, "but for security's sake I will close the door."

"Well, some of the servants have said," continued Jerome— "don't be terrified, my good master, that it is your father come to give you back your right; for they say the castle ought to be yours; why to be sure, I say to them, it seems so; but there may be reasons why it should not. I say no more to *them:* now, my good master, I have often thought in my own mind, that you are no relation of the baron of Ollada."

"How!" cried Altador, "is the present baron Garcia then an impostor?"

"Oh! no, no," exclaimed the old man, "but I think the former baron was no more your father than he was mine; I know not why, but he never loved you as he would have done, had you been his child: now it was no business of mine, but many a time in my heart I pitied you; poor child, said I to myself, he is born to bear all dame Fortune's surly buffets! I always loved you, for you were a sweet-tempered babe."

"But who then do you think this ghost may be?" asked Altador.

"You have heard, I suppose," replied Jerome, "that the lady Hypolita once had a husband."

"I have," returned Altador.

"Well, his name was don Gomez de Castro, a worthy gentleman as any you shall meet with in all Toledo, but somewhat addicted to gaming; well, it was given out that he was in debt to the present baron of Ollada, more than he could pay him, and so hanged himself in despair; he was then at the castle. Well, I blame no one—it is no business of mine, but thoughts are free."

"I understand what you would insinuate," replied Altador, "but from the many accounts I have heard of his death, and even

47

from the lady Hypolita herself, all of which so exactly tally, I must hope your conjecture is without foundation:—but did you ever see this walking spirit before last night?"

"Ay, my good master, one cold bleak night, when I pitied the poor suffering ghost from my soul, and Villetta and Lopez both saw it, but he was fain to laugh it off then too; I saw how it was, and so I said nothing about it, it was no business of mine, and so it was all hushed up; and I thought perhaps it might have walked its time and was quieted; but no, last night it came again, and terrified us all so, that we determined to tell the baron of it, and that we would all leave him if he did not get it laid."

"But supposing there should be a spirit," cried Altador, "as it does not come within the mansion, what can you have to fear from it?"

"Ah!" replied the old man, "you would not say so if you knew all I know; nobody knows what I do but myself; I have never mentioned it, for I thought I should only get laughed at, or perhaps affronted by the baron, so I said nothing; but I'll tell you, for I know I may trust you—may I not, my good master?"

"You may indeed," said Altador.

"Well, the first time that Villetta and I saw it, I had been to my sister's, and I saw it as I was coming across the lawn home again; we were very much frightened, both of us; so when we were composed a little, we went to bed, for Lopez and she had sat up for me; so, as my room looks the other way, and I had a great mind to see whether it was gone, I thought I would cross the narrow gallery, and steal up the left hand stairs, and take a peep out of the great window by the side of the portal, that looks straight upon the green; so I got there safe enough, and then I thought I would cast a look round to see if any body was watching me, or any thing; and as I looked towards the flight of stairs on the right, I saw the ghost creeping up as softly—I began to tremble, oh! holy Maria! what a fright I was in! and it glided along till it came to the lady Hypolita's door, and there it stopped; mark that, my good master; but it never looked at me, and so I thought I would e'en get away as fast as I could; but as I was going down stairs, I saw it go on to the baron's chamber door, and there it stopped again;—I warrant he trembled sorely enough, if he would own it; well, there I left it, and I ran to my own bed directly."

"But how could you distinguish any thing in the dark?"

"Oh! I took my lamp with me to light me up stairs, my good master, but the moon had just burst from under a cloud, and so I put out the lamp, lest any one should discover me by it, and the moon shining, in at the square window that fronts the gallery, served to shew me the spirit. Ah! my good master, long have I wished for some one that I could safely trust this dismal story with, for it hath laboured sorely for utterance, and Heaven of its bounty hath sent me thee; my heart is easier now I have told you of it, so farewell; we must not be seen long together, lest we be suspected; in times like these, suspicion breeds fast."

"Thou sayest true, old man, and thou mayest rest assured, that the confidence which thou hast put in me, is not misplaced."

"Pray the Virgin no evil come of what I have been saying."

"Never fear, good Jerome," answered Altador, and they then separated.

CHAPTER VI

Oh! world, thy slippery turns! friends now fast sworn,
Whose double bosoms seem to wear one heart:
Whose hours, whose bed, whose meal, and exercise,
Are still together; who twine (as 'twere) in love
Inseparable, shall within this hour,
On a dissension of a doit, break out
To bitterest enmity. So fellest foes,
Whose passions and whose plots have broke their sleep,
To take the one, the other, by some chance,
Some trick, not worth an egg, shall grow dear friends
And interjoin their issues.

CORIOLANUS

No sooner was breakfast ended, than the baron commanded Lopez to inform the domestics, that he should not go to the castle until the expiration of another hour; this was a respite joyfully received by them, and earnestly did they hope it might be extended to a general pardon.

The lady Hypolita and Altador had retired to the garden; the baron had commanded his daughter to remain with him, as he had something of importance to communicate to her.

Altador informed the lady Hypolita of all that he had heard that morning, save Jerome's conjecture concerning her husband, don Gomez, which he from delicacy omitted; and Hypolita, in return, acquainted him with the conversation that had passed between Matilda and Villetta, the preceding night, which Matilda had related to her during the confusion in the hall; and she concluded by advising him, at all events, to accompany the baron, his uncle, to the castle that morning, and strictly to observe his every look when there.

They had now been in the garden for about half-an-hour, when a servant summoned Altador immediately to attend his uncle; the lady Hypolita and he accordingly moved towards the mansion. Altador entered the baron's study; the lady Hypolita perceiving that Matilda was not in the apartment where she had left her, inquired of Flora, whom she met in the hall, whether Matilda was walking in the garden; and being answered that she was in her own chamber, she instantly repaired thither.

What was her surprise on opening the door, to behold Matilda lying seemingly lifeless on the bed, and Villetta standing by her, administering water with a very bountiful hand; on seeing Hypolita, she exclaimed—"Oh! my lady, I am glad you are come; I durst not leave my mistress to come and call you, but if wishing could have brought you, I wished for you enough, I am sure."

"What has been the matter?" asked Hypolita.

"Oh! my lady, I scarcely know any more than you; but I fear my mistress is dying."

"No, no," answered Hypolita, "don't be alarmed, she is only in a fainting fit; open the window, and leave her quite alone."

"Shan't I unlace her stays, my lady?"

"There is no occasion; but can't you tell what has so deeply affected her?"

"Why, my lady, I don't know whether I can or not hardly; but just now, I thought the lady Matilda had been alone, and I was going to ask her, just to ask my lord to excuse Lopez going to the castle to help to look for the spirit: I suppose you have heard the fright we were all in, about the ghost last night, my lady?"

"Yes, I have."

"Well, my lady, so when I got to the door—Oh! poor soul, how she jerks about! nip her hand a little harder, my lady; Lopez nipped mine so hard when I was frightened at the ghost in the winter, that I often think I feel it to this day—so when I got to the door, my lady, as I was saying, I heard my lord say, as loud as he could speak—'You shall marry him the day after to-morrow.' I an't quite certain whether those were the words; but however, they were to that purpose; and so then I heard my lady say—I verily believe she was on her knees, poor soul, as much as that my lord had promised her he never would force her to marry any body; so then the baron said a great deal about rank, and fortune, and grandeur, and titles, and such things; and then, says he—'To be a duchess, the duchess of Gonsalez.'"

"Gracious Heaven!" interrupted Hypolita, "are you certain he made use of these words?"

"Oh, yes, my lady; for I said to myself, 'Villetta,' says I, 'if your lady gets to be a duchess, not but that she is good enough to be a queen, she will turn you off, I warrant you.' Well, my lady, but that has nothing to do with what I was saying; so my lord said, says he—no, my lady said—'I can never be happy and comfortable with him,' says she; so says my lord—'I'll try that when Altador is gone; he shan't be in the way much longer,'—as much as to say, the lady Matilda was fond of him, but whether she is or not, I am sure I can't tell; and then the baron rang the bell, and so I ran away, for fear they should see me listening; and, indeed, my lady, I should not have listened, if it had not been as I told you; and so my mistress came up stairs and began to cry, and threw herself on the bed, as you see her, and there she has lain ever since; that is all I can tell you, my lady."

"I have heard enough," cried Hypolita, as the silent tear stole down her cheek; "but see, Matilda revives; leave us, Villetta."

"Perhaps the lady Matilda would like a little wine, or something, before I go; won't you ask her, my lady?"

"If I should want any thing I'll ring," said Hypolita, and Villetta then left the chamber, though with visible reluctance.

Matilda now raised her head, and exclaiming—"Oh! madam," burst into tears, which for a long time prevented her utterance— "Oh! cruel, cruel father," continued she, "what have I done to merit such a punishment? Oh! my dearest madam—the duke— the hated Gaspero—I cannot name it."

"I know what thou wouldst say, my dearest child," returned the affectionate Hypolita; "but summon thy fortitude; the interposing hand of Heaven may still deliver thee; and if thou must submit, murmur not, for it is a father who commands."

"But, oh! my dearest mother," cried Matilda, "for you are a mother to me, am not I also his child, and have I not studied every wish of his? conformed myself unto his will, even with the most rigorous nicety? wept with anxious fondness over his sick bed, and wearied Heaven and all the saints with my unceasing prayers for his recovery? Did I not mourn, when obliged to fly from him, and bless the hour that brought me back to his embraces? have I not in all these respects acted as became a child, a dutiful child? and does he now forget he is a father, and sacrifice that child to age, brutality, and lust?—the stroke is too heavy for my sinking heart."

"Mitigate these transports, my love," replied Hypolita, "it is not ours to make election for ourselves; by the custom of our country, fathers must decide our fate; I have known the curse of disobedience to a father's will, and learnt, too late, alas! that seeming resignation is our kindest friend."

"But why, my dearest madam," asked Matilda, "why was I taught to flatter myself with the delusive hope, that my choice would be free? an indulgence rarely granted to our countrywomen, and therefore the more highly did I prize it, as a mark of love from an affectionate parent: oh! wherefore was this?"

"What you ask, my child," returned Hypolita, "I cannot answer; certain it is, that an impenetrable mystery has for some time clouded your father's actions; some secret spring actuates his conduct, I am well assured."

Matilda now revealed to the lady Hypolita her love for the young peasant, at the same time enjoining her to secresy: the lady Hypolita, with a smile, told her, that she had perceived the growing flame with great anxiety, and had intended taking the first opportunity of setting before her the imprudence of it, and representing to her the great improbability of her father's ever giving his consent to her bestowing her hand on a man of his low rank in life, even if the duke of Gonsalez had never urged his suit.

"Oh! madam," cried Matilda, "he is not what he seems; nay, you yourself heard him affirm that he was not; and if he were, has he not virtues that entitle him to a princess's love?"

"You know him but imperfectly, my child; how are you certain that he has not imposed on your credulity?"

"Would he then have exposed his life for my safety?" asked Matilda.

"His honour would not suffer him to see a helpless woman assaulted," answered Hypolita.

"And that honour," cried Matilda, "forbade him to *deceive* a helpless woman; methinks his eyes told me he would have gloried in dying for me; oh! madam, they pierced me to the heart; I could have told him how I loved him, and though an humble cottager, have blessed my lucky stars that threw him in my way, and been content to feed my flocks with his upon the mountains, if he but smiled to recompense me for my labour."

"By the Holy Virgin I entreat you," said Hypolita, "let not these idle thoughts, which finally, I fear, must end in your father's warmest resentment, obtain so strong dominion over you: but tell me, said the baron nought concerning Altador?"

"He charged me with loving him, named him as the bar between me and the duke, and declared, that unless I would consent to wed Gaspero, Altador should be removed far distant from Ollada."

"What answer made you to this?" eagerly inquired the lady Hypolita.

"I was silent, and my father immediately left the room.—I know what you are going to say," continued Matilda, interrupting Hypolita, who was beginning to address her, "I know what you are going to say, and I answer you, that I love Altador as a brother, I respect him as a friend, but I cannot regard him as my husband—for pity, urge me not concerning him! Alas! the baron is unconscious that Altador must not, cannot be mine! Question me not, I entreat you, concerning what I have said: my faith is pledged not to reveal what I know, and I fear I have now said too much: would I might say more to you, my dearest lady, but it must not be."

She now turned to the window, her lovely cheeks again bedewed with tears; while the lady Hypolita continued on her seat, motionless with surprise.

Altador, on entering his uncle's study, was thus addressed by him.—"You see, my dearest Altador, that in order to secure peace in my house, I am under the necessity of satisfying the domestics whether or no there be a spirit resident in the deserted Castle of Ollada, and I have promised to go with them thither this morning; and as on account of my indisposition, which you know has confined me until these two last days, I have not had an opportunity of clearing those suspicions, which the words I uttered in my delirium must naturally have raised in you, I would wish you now to accompany me, and by exploring every part of the castle, together with me, clear away any doubts which may still remain in your breast."

"If I ever did entertain any suspicions," answered Altador, "which from my conduct, my lord, I think you have no reason to imagine, a visit to the castle together with you, will by no means lessen them."

The baron, affecting not to understand him, cried—"Pardon me, Altador, I did not mean to accuse you wrongfully; may I hope for your attendance?"

"I will accompany you, my lord."

The baron now directed Lopez to command the servants to follow him; adding, that with regard to the females, he left it entirely to their option whether to go or not; and they then proceeded towards the portal; the servants, headed by Lopez, followed at an awful distance, with countenances not less piteous than if they had been going to their execution. They were now arrived without the mansion, when Villetta, rushing past them, fell on her knees before the baron, exclaiming—"Oh! my lord, I hope you won't be angry, my lord—thank you humbly for excusing me, my lord—but pray don't be angry, my lord—Lopez, my lord—one man can't make much difference; must he—mayn't he be excused, my lord?"

"I excuse no one," answered the baron; "does Lopez then refuse to go? if so, he quits my service."

"Who, I my lord?" cried Lopez, advancing, "I refuse to follow your lordship any where?"

"Now, Lopez," interrupted Villetta, "how obstinate you are, that you won't be afraid of the spirit!" and burst into tears.

"Come on, Lopez," said Garcia, "and pay no attention to a silly girl's whining."

"I don't, my lord, I don't," replied Lopez. "Don't cry, you silly fool," continued he, turning to Villetta; "I shall come back safe enough, I promise you." Then beginning to whistle, as regardless of what she said, he again placed himself in the van, and the melancholy troop once more proceeded on their march.

Being arrived on the eastern side of the castle, where that which had once been a moat was in some parts still discernible, they passed over a decayed drawbridge, and crossing a court nearly choked with weeds, they entered the lofty chequered hall, and proceeded to a flight of stairs which faced them.—"Shall we ascend these stairs?" said the baron.

"Just which way your lordship pleases," answered all the servants with one voice; and they again set forward.

They now entered a gallery, which Altador conjectured to run parallel with that where he had so unfortunately lost his friends a few nights before, but it was in a far more ruinous state than that on the northern side. Their entrance caused no small alarm to a haunt of bats, who had here taken up their abode, and no less terror to the servants, who began scampering down stairs as fast as they were able, but were soon recalled by the baron's threats. This uproar being somewhat allayed, they entered a door on the left; it opened into an apartment in which former magnificence was still visible through layers of cobwebs; it was adorned with portraits, the faces of which were rendered indistinguishable from the accumulated dust of a length of years; the windows, being of coloured glass, and also clouded with dirt, added a dim and fiery light, more terrible than the thickest darkness; the ponderous marble slabs had crushed the gilded frames, which once had afforded them an able support, and lay cracked amidst the ruins they themselves had made; the hangings were of an orange-coloured velvet; the chairs, which were composed of the same material, were become prey to the worms, and not one of them was remaining in an upright position: from this apartment followed a suite of rooms, some of which had been decorated with princely magnificence, others fitted up in a style simply elegant; the last of these was a bedchamber, in which there were two closets.—"Open those doors," said the baron; "let us be certain, ere we leave this part of the castle, that the spirit has not hidden himself in one of these."

Lopez pulled back one of the doors, and opened to view a neat closet, in which hung a decayed lute, and on a small table stood an ivory inkstand, which powdered at the touch: this Altador conjectured to have been the chamber of his mother, and he envied those instruments that they once had belonged to her; he wished to ask them of the baron, but something, he knew not what, warned him not to mention the unfortunate Fatima.

"Open the other door," said the baron; his orders were obeyed, and Altador was awakened from the trance into which he had fallen, by the shrieking of the servants, who were running, some one way, some another. Jerome, as was his usual custom when terrified, had fallen on his knees, and begun to pray; Pedro was exclaiming without ceasing—"That is it, that is it, just as I beheld it the other night—that is it." Altador now found that this alarm had been occasioned by the flight of an owl from her daily haunt, who had been roused by the opening of the closet door: some time was passed before all the servants had summoned sufficient courage to return, but at length, impelled rather by the baron's menaces than their own increasing fortitude, they re-entered the gallery.

They now repaired to the western gallery, and having passed through all the apartments that bordered on it without any particular alarm, they proceeded to that on the northern side. Altador's sensations were now disagreeable beyond conception, all the occurrences of that fatal night were present to his thoughts, and he had scarcely strength to proceed. They were now arrived at Ferdinand's study.—"There, Altador," exclaimed the baron, "are the portraits of your grandfather Carlos, and your grandmother Joanna; I have not removed them to my mansion, being very imperfect likenesses of those whom they are intended to represent."

Whilst Garcia was speaking, Jerome pointed significantly to the closet at the end of this suite of apartments, then to his own neck, and shook his head, his eyes all the time fixed on Altador, who conjectured that he wished to inform him, that it was there the husband of the lady Hypolita had hanged himself; nor did he misinterpret the old man's signs; they now proceeded towards it, and being arrived there, Altador cast his eyes minutely over every part of the wainscot and floor, but could not perceive the smallest crevice, or any appearance of an outlet; they then crossed the angle of the castle, and entered the eastern gallery: this part of the edifice did not appear ever to have been fitted up, and Garcia informed him that it never had been inhabited, assigning as a reason, the largeness of the building, and unnecessary expence of furnishing so vast a number of apartments, which could never, on any occasion whatsoever, have been all in use at the same time.

Being descended into the hall, the baron asked whether they were satisfied with their search? They were all silent, and he repeated the question.—"Might not we as well take a look in there?" said Jerome, pointing to a large pair of folding doors, at the extremity of the hall.

"Oh, certainly," answered the baron.

Lopez opened the doors, and they beheld a kitchen, in which many culinary implements lay dispersed upon the dressers and tables; the fire-place was in disorder; logs of wood lay scattered about the hearth, and a kettle was hanging over the iron bars, made to support the wood fire.

"The ghost seems to live well," said Lopez.

"What, on rusty pans and kettles?" cried Pedro; "no, poor spirit, his heart is too full to eat, I warrant him."

"A truce to this idle prating," exclaimed the baron; "those who do not wish to be locked up in the castle follow me."

This order he had no occasion to repeat; the whole troop ran to the door immediately, and the baron having locked the heavy gates, studded with iron knobs, returned the rusty key into his pocket, and they all descended the steps.

"Thank Heaven, we have escaped!" cried Pedro.

"Holy Maria be praised!" said Jerome.

"I shall expect," said the baron, "since I have condescended to convince you of the idleness of your fears, to hear no more complaints, similar to those which were brought me this morning.— Are you all satisfied that your alarm was without cause?"

"Why, my lord," answered Jerome, "it was not very likely we should find any thing by day—a spirit, you know, never walks but in the night time."

"Ay, very true, Jerome—very true," exclaimed several of the servants.

"Curse on these fools!" cried the baron; "but I will go one step farther, to convince them if possible: has any one of you a desire to pass the night in watching in the castle? if any one wishes so to do, let him now declare it—he has my consent."

"May three of us go, pray your lordship?" asked Antonio, who had shewn less fear than the rest, save Lopez.

"For your purpose, one is as good as three," answered the baron; "however, I shall suffer no more than one to watch—does any one choose to undertake the business?"

They were all silent.

"As no one answers," continued the baron, "I find no one has sufficient resolution; now remember, I listen to no more tales, the effect of your chicken hearts; proceed to the mansion, Altador and myself will follow."

CHAPTER VII

——————In such a night as this,
When the sweet wind did gently kiss the trees,
And they did make no noise; in such a night,
Troilus, methinks, mounted the Trojan walls,
And sighed his soul towards the Grecian tents,
Where Cressid lay that night.

Merchant of Venice.

....

I swear to thee by Cupid's strongest bow,
By his best arrow with the golden head,
By the simplicity of Venus' doves,
By that which knitteth souls, and prospers loves,
And by that fire, which burn'd the Carthage queen
When the false Trojan under sail was seen,
By all the vows that ever men have broke,
In number more than women ever spoke,
In that same place thou hast appointed me,
To-morrow truly will I meet with thee.

A Midsummer Night's Dream.

ALTADOR, on his return to the mansion, was sought by the lady Hypolita, who acquainted him with what had passed between the baron and Matilda; nor did she omit telling him his uncle's intention concerning him, of which the baron had made no mention to him; nor had he even acquainted him with his daughter's intended marriage.

The day was passed in silent grief by every one, except Garcia, who laughed, talked, sang, drank frequent goblets of wine tilled to the brim, and at times appeared deranged in his mind, but immediately recovered himself.

Night at length arrived, and they retired to their chambers; Matilda was accompanied by Villetta, who again made the same request she had advanced with success the prior evening; but Matilda insisted on her sleeping in her own chamber.

Matilda, when alone, opened the casement; it was one of the most beautiful nights she had ever beheld, and as her mind was too ill at ease to suffer her to compose herself to sleep, she determined to pass away the night in a small grove, which was encircled by a wall at the back of the mansion; accordingly, when she imagined all the family to be at rest, she descended, and having unbolted the doors with little difficulty, she entered the grove.

This was a night that seemed to rival mid-day; the silver shadow of the moon swam upon the glassy surface of a small rivulet, that ran winding through a knot of lofty elms, around whose barky trunks, in fragrant wreaths, entwined itself the luscious honeysuckle, and sweet-scented eglantine; not far from these, a venerable oak, whose deep engrafted roots had long defied the wintry gusts, stood monarch of the shady grove, illumined by the moon's reflected beams, upon the pearly drops of brightest dew, that studded its silky leaves: underneath, upon a mossy bed, perfumed by violets and thyme, where wide-spreading jasmine extended a light canopy, Matilda chose her seat; and the gentle breeze that played beneath the umbrageous boughs, fanned her white bosom, panting with heat.

She reclined her head upon her hand, and throwing back her loosely flowing garment, that she might the more freely taste the refreshing zephyr, sunk slowly down upon the velvet turf; her thoughts wandered, first to the detested duke, and she felt in the strongest manner all the disgust that the idea of being forced into the arms of a man whom she despised could inspire; they then passed to him, whom her luxuriant fancy had drawn more perfect, more transcendent o'er his sex, than nature ever yet produced a mortal; she sighed, she wept, she wished him now before her, and yet she feared to see him; it was a moment when love filled up each vacant crevice of her heart, and she longed to throw herself upon the protection of him who had kindled the sacred flame.

She was awakened from the trance into which she had fallen, by the clock at the monastery, which now proclaimed the midnight hour. She raised her head, and casting her eyes around, perceived some one walking slowly along near the mansion; the reports which she had heard concerning a spirit, the hour of the night, her solitary situation, all conspired to heighten her alarm; suddenly she rose from the spot where she had been seated; the figure now turned an angle formed by a cloister of shrubs, and the moon shining bright upon the place where it stood, she discovered the young peasant; falling on his knees before her, and seizing her hand, he exclaimed—"Forgive, most honoured lady, this interruption of your meditations, from one, whom you as yet know but imperfectly; but, oh! lady, there is no one takes a truer interest in thy welfare, than he whom thou hast bound to thee by the very heart of friendship, by the most sacred bonds of love."

"Imprudent that you are!" cried Matilda, as he pressed her hand to his lips, with unrestrained transport, "why have you ventured here at such an hour? should any one, should my father behold you thus, I tremble at the consequences that might ensue; rise, I conjure you, rise."

"Say you do not hate me then, lady; but I merit your warmest resentment. Oh! speak then, if it be but to declare you *do* hate me, for to be *hated* by you, I must sometimes be in your thoughts; that were to me a soothing consolation; if you neither loved nor hated me, oblivion soon would fill the slender vacancy I pant to hold in your thoughts; yet trust me, lady, from this your silence, I hear you speak a gentle welcome. Am I deceived in this, my fondest hope?"

"Alas!" returned Matilda, "how can I welcome him, whose safety is tenfold dearer to me than all I prize beside, at such a time when every danger hovers round him? Fly, I entreat you; should my despotic father discover you here, though he were told the simple truth, of all that ere has passed between us, his wrath would paint it in the colour of a falsehood, and his vengeance pursue the innocent, though suspected perpetrators."

"Banish all apprehension of discovery from the baron Garcia; by my veracity, I swear that thou hast nought to fear from him; though I cannot now explain unto thee how I became acquainted with it, yet I have most certain knowledge that he will not break in upon us; he has affairs of weightier importance to turn his thoughts unto."

"You talk to me in riddles," replied Matilda; "unravel them, and I will give you patient hearing."

"I cannot now, my dearest love, for I must call thee mine; my time admits not of delay; hear then the purport of my rude intrusion; it was love that urged me to it, lady; therefore, if I have erred, pronounce a gentle punishment on me, since 'twas in blindness of affection that I have been, perhaps, mistakenly officious."

"I seal thy pardon without hesitation, for well am I assured that thy intent, whatever it be, is nobly formed; but, oh! proceed, and calm the anxious fears and doubts, that rise like waves, successive in my fluttering heart."

"Suffice it then to tell you, dearest love, that well acquainted with your father's rash intention of surrendering you unto the lustful Gaspero, I now venture to offer you an asylum, where you will be safely guarded from the duke, and your father the baron. Will you then condescend to put yourself under my protection? I swear unto you by——"

"Nay, swear not," interrupted Matilda; "I must believe whatever thou speakest."

"Sweetest fair," returned the young peasant, "say then that thou wilt put still greater faith in me, and meet me here tomorrow night at twelve; if I live, I will be here, and carry thee beyond the reach of those who would basely make traffic of thee."

"Alas! thy honeyed accents steal to my inmost heart, and tempt me to give fullest credit to all that thou sayest."

"Then thou wilt meet me?"

"To say I will, were to say, that I can read futurity's vast volume, and pronounce whatever will happen; but, by the gratitude I owe thy former services, if nought do place a bar irremovable between us, I promise thee that thou shalt find me here."

"Oh! blessed, blessed words! sure my senses are deceived, and all that passes now before me is but a vision; repeat thy words, let the glad sounds once more, in sweetest repetition, vibrate on my ear."

"Distrust me not—to-morrow night shall prove my truth."

"May Heaven prosper thy endeavours! permit me, lady, to seal a mutual promise of our faith upon thy lips. And now, farewell; may the protectors of fair innocence cloak thee from every harm till my return."

"Heaven defend thee!" cried Matilda.

The young peasant, then casting back a farewell look, ran hastily along the smooth-cut grass, and scaling the wall with the nimblest agility, was in an instant shut from the eyes of the happy and astonished Matilda.

In the morning, Altador was shut up with the baron in his study for nearly an hour; when his uncle informed him, that he wished him to make the necessary preparations for returning to the monastery of Cordova, in the course of two days, without assigning any reason for his conduct.

Altador determined to take the earliest opportunity of urging his suit with Matilda, and endeavouring to prevail with her to intercede with the baron in his behalf; for Hypolita, at Matilda's particular request, had not mentioned to him the hints which Matilda had dropped, concerning the impossibility of Altador's ever becoming her husband; he avoided seeing Hypolita alone, lest she should caution him against a declaration of his passion.

Matilda retired to her apartment at an early hour, and having collected all her trinkets of value, not knowing to what extremities she might be reduced by unforeseen accidents, she enclosed them all in a small casket, and carefully deposited them in her pocket; she now sat ruminating on what might be her future state—about to trust herself with a man of whom she had no knowledge whatsoever, but the seemingly great goodness of his heart and his faithful love; and how was she certain that *those* were not formed to deceive her? but no, she loved him too fondly to admit the idea, even for a moment, and her fancy presented none but pleasing prospects to her view: the moon shone bright; she placed herself before the window, and cast her eyes in mournful silence over the spot where she had passed her early life in joys uninterrupted; it was perhaps the last time she should ever behold it; at this thought the crystal tears fell fast from her swelling eyes; she felt a reluctance to bid farewell, even to her chamber, but her eternal welfare depended on this moment: she once more cast her eyes hastily around, and entered the gallery; she listened—all was silent; she descended into the hall; she again stopped—all was still; she now ventured to unbolt the door—she effected it without the least noise, and at length congratulated herself on her safe arrival in the grove. The moon was at this time hidden under a dark cloud; she had not waited many minutes ere she imagined she heard footsteps; she listened attentively— they seemed to recede from the spot where she stood—she flew towards the sound—she turned an angle of the grove, and saw a youth, whom she could not doubt to be the young peasant, walking slowly with his back towards her; she coughed as loud as she durst, from the fear of being overheard; he turned round his head immediately, he advanced quickly towards her, and she with swift steps flew to meet him; the moon at that instant burst from under a cloud, and to her inexpressible astonishment, she perceived on his knees before her, Altador.

END OF VOLUME ONE

The Castle of Ollada

Volume II

CHAPTER I

What stronger breastplate than a heart untainted!
Thrice is he arm'd who hath his quarrel just;
And he but naked (tho' lock'd up in steel),
Whose conscience with injustice is corrupted.

Second Part of Henry VI.

"MATILDA!" exclaimed Altador, "oh! say what blessed chance, propitious to my most exalted wishes, hath sent thee hither?"

Matilda, somewhat recovered from her surprise, replied, "Rise, Altador, and hear me."

"Though to lie prostrate at Matilda's feet, were bliss beyond compare, yet it were a crime still greater, not to yield obedience implicit unto her commands—I rise, fair fair lady."

"If such [be] your sentiments," returned Matilda, "it is unnecessary for me to say more, than that I wish to be alone."

"Were I well certified," answered Altador, "that solitude was what Matilda sought, I'd fly the world ere I thus rudely would intrude on her retirement; but is there not—(pardon me, dearest Matilda, that I question you thus minutely—my peace of mind most nearly is concerned), is there not?—Oh! answer me, for I am well assured that thou divinest what I would ask."

"Will it suffice that I declare unto thee, I can never be thine?"

"Oh! my prophetic heart—Matilda!—why have you?—could you not?"

"Let me now entreat you," cried Matilda, "instantly to leave me; you must not stay—indeed you must not, Altador."

"One instant hear me, and the wretched Altador never more will interrupt the moment dedicated to a rival's triumph! Think not, Matilda, that I mean to upbraid thee for loving another; may the man on whom thou deignest to smile, be worthier of thee, than he, whom this thy recent declaration driveth to despair; yet, ere I go, answer me, candidly answer me. Has the ardour, which at an early period of our lives, I strove by every means within the narrow compass of my limited abilities to evince for you, and which you seemed to answer with a smile of love reciprocal, has it ever, in any the smallest degree, abated? nay, Heaven is my witness, that when absent from you, my thoughts have never strayed one instant from your loved idea; and was it, Matilda, a grateful return for never wandering love, to fix your heart upon a peasant youth, whom chance first set before your eyes?"

"I plainly perceive," returned Matilda, "that you are acquainted with the inmost secrets of my heart; how you have gained the knowledge of them, I have yet to learn; I chide you not for your reproaches: had I idly, as you suppose, and justly I confess, transferred my love from him, for whom I once avowed the most unfeigned affection, to one of whom I have but slender cognizance, without a cause, save the giddy impulse of an unwary moment, to have been driven from earth by blasts of lightning, had been a punishment inadequate to my deserts; I'll tell thee then, that I still love thee, not with less fondness than when first I listened, all enraptured, to thy tale of love; I own, that then I nourished the fond hope, that you, in course of time, would be my lawful spouse; but the all-seeing eye of Providence, a witness to a flame, which, if pursued, inevitably must have plunged us both in misery eternal, disclosed to me, by its all-wise direction, a fatal secret, which I have sworn never to reveal, save on the greatest exigency: let thy reason teach thee not to require an explanation of my words; my oath is past, and a trust so sacred I will not violate; esteem me—regard me as thy warmest friend—but cease to love me as——Oh! fly," continued she, "I beseech you fly, or I am lost for ever."

Altador now instinctively turned his eyes the way which Matilda's were bent, and perceived a man at some distance, advancing towards them. "Must I then," exclaimed he, "must I resign thee to a rival's arms?"

"By Heaven," returned Matilda, "thou hast no rival in the love I bear thee."

"Gracious God," cried Altador, his eyes still rivetted on the advancing person, "knowest thou who it is that now approacheth?"

"Perplex me not with these inquiries; when we meet again, thou shalt know all; yield me now, I entreat you, to him, who at this time is alone able to afford me protection."

"Thou ravest, Matilda," returned Altador; "it is thy father who advanceth."

"Blessed Virgin succour me, my father! then I am lost indeed," cried Matilda, and sunk lifeless into Altador's arms.

"What have I done?" cried he; "oh! Heaven assist her."

"Call on that Heaven to assist thyself," exclaimed the baron, "for thou shalt need its help to escape my just resentment."

"Of what crime, my lord," asked Altador, with as great composure as he could command, "have I been guilty, to merit such an exclamation?"

"Resolute villain," returned the baron, "dost think to trifle with me? or dost suppose me such a novice in the crafty ways of men, that my slender penetration cannot fathom e'en the wiles of love-sick striplings? forego my daughter."

"My lord," said Altador, "the———"

"No words," returned the baron; "retire to thine own chamber, and by six meet me in my study." So saying, he snatched Matilda in his arms, and moved towards the mansion; having entered the hall, and locked the door, the key of which he secured in the pocket of his under garment, he repeated his commands to Altador, and proceeded with Matilda to her chamber; having laid her upon the bed, and perceiving that her senses were returning, he closed the door, left her, and immediately retired to his own apartment.

About the hour of eight on the succeeding morning, the baron re-entered the chamber of the desponding Matilda. "I come not," cried he, "to reproach thee for the transactions of yesternight, nor to forbid a repetition of them—that were unnecessary. Thy minion, Altador, is by this time far removed from hence; I have myself seen him a league on his road towards the monastery of Cordova."

"Oh! my father," returned Matilda, the tears bursting afresh from her eyes, "why have you so cruelly treated one who never was in fault?"

"In thy deluded sight I freely can believe he never erred," exclaimed the baron, his contracted brow relaxing into a satyrical smile.

"By the God of all mercies," cried Matilda, "it was chance that led us both to the same spot; here on my knees I swear, that were you, my father, now to offer him unto me with your fullest approbation, I would refuse his hand."

"Convince me of the truth of this assertion," replied the baron, "by instantly receiving that of the duke. This night I hold a sumptuous banquet; see that thou attend it with becoming gaiety."

"Alas! my father," said Matilda, "I cannot wear a face of smiles when it is at variance with my heart. But remember, sir, if you force me to his hated arms, I seek protection at the altar."

"The altar may not, cannot, shall not screen thee from a father's vengeance."

"Be it so," cried Matilda, with increasing firmness; "I have still one friend left, that will not fail to afford me an uninterrupted asylum; the grave never yet refused protection to a persecuted child, against a cruel father's unprovoked resentment."

"Romantic girl," returned the baron, "beware, lest I try thy boasted resolution."

"You are a Spaniard, sir," cried Matilda, "and it is your nature to be firm in your resolution; I am your daughter, sir—why should not I inherit that firmness?—You'll say, because I am a woman; and has a woman then no right to plead in her defence? must she be sold, sacrificed, made traffic of, without the liberty to say she is wronged, or to assert those rights which nature gave to all? I'll call on all the powers of Heaven and earth to vindicate my cause."

"On earth," replied the baron, "thou wilt find few who will oppose a father's right; call not on Heaven, thou hast already drawn its vengeance on thee by disobedience to a father's will."

"Heaven," cried the lovely maid, "is just, and whilst it sees that the commands of parents are so, its wrath never fails to overtake filial disobedience; but when on the restricted privileges allowed them, parents usurp unlimited authority for the most unjustifiable purposes, Providence never neglects to interpose in their behalf, and to that Providence I resign me."

"See thou attend at the banquet," exclaimed the baron, seemingly choking with rage, and instantly left the apartment.

Matilda now sought the lady Hypolita, and informed her of all that had passed. Hypolita sympathized in her distress, and gave her such consolation as she was able, though she could not help blaming her for the imprudent step she had been about to take without consulting her, who she was well assured would have advised her only for her good.

Evening being arrived, Matilda entered the festive hall, habited in white, an emblem of her innocence; and her auburn locks were adorned with leaves of the olive, of a pale green colour, as when they first shoot out from the stem in the infancy of spring. The pillared hall rang with the cheering sounds of various instruments; the knights led the ladies through the mazes of the animating dance, and Matilda was constrained to give her hand to the man who had attempted the violation of her honour.

They were now seated at the banquet, and a health to Matilda went round in an overflowing goblet of wine.

The minstrels sang the verses which celebrated the deeds of the most renowned knights in battle, and the gallant feats of the Spaniards against the Infidels in the land of Palestine, where the rude Saracen opposed the horned crescent to the holy cross. The breasts of the knights present were warmed by the heroic conduct of the champions of their faith; they wished for a renewal of those noble exploits, and they requested the baron to suffer a tournament to be held on the following day; to this petition he readily agreed; and Gaspero immediately rose, and offered himself to oppose any champions who might present themselves. At a late hour the feast broke up.

In the morning of the following day, the knights all appeared upon a spot of even ground, which had been chosen for the purpose, in the front of the baron's mansion.

The duke of Gonsalez wore the most sumptuous apparel, and most gorgeous armour; he trusted to his strength and skill in arms to support him through the dangers of the day with success, and crown him with glory, and he panted to prove himself superior in arms, in the presence of his mistress. The ladies who honoured the solemnity with their presence, were assembled at the windows of Garcia's mansion.

The baron, attended by the chosen heralds, surveyed and limited the ground. The heralds then sounded their trumpets, and the duke of Gonsalez demanded admittance; the barriers were lifted up, and he entered, mounted on a steed of brightest bay, with flowing mane and tail, with ears up pricked, that seemed transportedly to catch the trumpet's bray, and spurn the earth he trod upon: Gaspero tempered his fiery spirit with the greatest judgment, and kept so firm a seat, that horse and rider seemed but one: his armour, of the finest workmanship, was formed by plates of polished steel, that overlaid each other in scales, whose edges were encrusted with silver, studded across the shoulders and round the collar with knobs of brightest gold: over this was thrown a lion's hide, of yellow hue; and the helmet resembled the head of that fierce animal, in whose front upreared nine plumes of fairest white, connected to the helmet by a band of precious stones, and a knot of silver tassels, blended with ribbands of a lively green, being the colours of his beautiful mistress; the fangs of the same formidable beast grinned horrid over his crest; the paws were extended over either shoulder, and the talons infixed in the hide were of massy gold: he was attended by two esquires, who bore, one his shield, the other his trusty lance: on the shield was painted a phœnix, rising from the flames; the motto—"I rose from flames—beware my fire;" his lance was of strongest box, with a point of steel, well tried in many a doubtful conflict.

His striking appearance and manly deportment gained him the applause of the assembled crowd; nor were they deceived in him; by skill and valour he unhorsed and vanquished all the opponent knights who ventured to contend with him, and swept away the entire honours of the contested field.

Matilda, and her faithful friend, the lady Hypolita, were the only spectators present, who did not behold this addition to his glory with an enraptured eye. Matilda plainly perceived his natural self-sufficiency, at every instant ready to break out from under a cloud of affected modesty and humility, which he endeavoured to draw over it. How ardently did she wish the pretended peasant to enter the lists, and by his valour, which in her idea was invincible, wrest from Gaspero the prize which was about to be adjudged to him! at that instant an esquire, with his beaver slouched, delivered him a billet in the following words:—

"The fame of the prowess of Gaspero hath excited the emulation of an unknown knight, who challengeth him to the lists on the morrow, when he shall be refreshed from the toils of this day, as the unknown knight wisheth not to take any the smallest advantage over the hitherto successful Gaspero."

The esquire who delivered these lines, instantly rode off.

"Thinks this unknown braggart," cried the duke, after he had perused the billet, his eyes flashing fire, "that I am weary with the gentle pastimes of this day? but be it as he wills it; he shows more wisdom than I looked for in such an upstart knave, in that he defers his disgrace unto the latest moment he is able."

The other knights whom Gaspero had vanquished, hearing him utter these words, which no one could help applying to himself, equally with the unknown knight, knew not how to contain that rage, which they had no means of shewing; and every one of them wished, not less earnestly than Matilda, that the unknown knight might sully the boasted reputation of the haughty Gaspero's valour in arms.

Long ere the rosy-fingered messenger of Phœbus had mounted her saffron car, and put to flight the morning star, still faintly twinkling, the esquires of the duke were busied in polishing his armour, dressing the trappings, and plaiting the pendant mane of his proud steed.

Gaspero lay sleepless on his ruffled bed, heaping heavy curses on the presumptuous wretch who dared aim at conquest over him; and he determined, if possible, to make the issue of the contest fatal to his detested rival.

The time for the combat being at hand, Gaspero entered the lists; the unknown knight shortly after arrived at the barriers, and demanded admittance; they were lifted up, and he rode in; he was mounted on a milk-white steed of highest mettle; his armour was of a bright black, without a single ornament, save three grey feathers in the front of his helmet, which corresponded in colour with his mantle; the impress of his shield was the sun sinking beneath the horizon; the motto—"I shall rise again;" he was attended by one esquire only. This was, to Matilda, a circumstance of much joy; she immediately pictured to herself the elder peasant in the esquire, and in the knight, him, whose image was never absent from her thoughts: how often, under the bare supposition of what she wished, did she pray to Heaven to guide his valiant arm to victory!

"If yours be the fortune of the day," exclaimed Gaspero, "you may well glory in having vanquished me; but if mine be the lot, what fame shall I acquire by overcoming one unknown, perhaps of little fame, or even of none in arms—tell me then thy name?"

The knight shook his head, and made a sign to prepare for the combat; they retired to some distance, spurred on their horses, and shivered their lances, without any injury being received on either side. For the second course, Gaspero placed his lance more firmly in the rest, and seemed resolved to give his antagonist the mortal blow; but the unknown knight warded this stroke with as great dexterity as he had done the former one, and again shivered his lance against the duke's shield. The trumpets now sounded to the third charge; Gaspero rushed desperately forward, and pitched his lance into his opponent's shield; Matilda gave an involuntary shriek. The knight, regardless of the additional weight he now had to bear, struck the duke so strong a blow, that he fell backward from his saddle, stunned by the shock.

"The Holy Mother of our Lord be praised!" cried Matilda, the tears of joy gushing from her sparkling eyes; and in an ecstacy, she kissed the little rosary that hung by her side.

The unknown knight now sprang from his steed, and tearing Matilda's colours from the helmet of the duke, and placing them on his own, again mounted his horse, and leaving the lists, galloped away, accompanied by his esquire.

The duke, who was entirely deprived of his senses, by the blow which fell on his helmet, was immediately conveyed to his own castle by his esquires.

Rage and disappointment choked the baron, and prevented him from giving utterance to his passionate thoughts.

Hypolita's feelings were consonant with those of Matilda, and *she* had acquired new life from the victory of the unknown knight, whom, from his success, she now more strongly than ever supposed to be the young peasant; all she lamented was, that he had not seized this favourable opportunity to discover himself; but then she considered, that it might have been contrary to his welfare so to have done; and that consideration checked her rising curiosity.

CHAPTER II

————————Of shapes that walk
At dead of night, and clank their chains.
                                    AKENSIDE

ALTADOR on being left by his uncle, determined not to go immediately to the monastery of Cordova, but to proceed to the cottage of old Hugo, his late nurse's husband, and request him to afford him shelter during the day, and at night to watch in the castle, as he now began to suspect that if the castle was infested, the beings who inhabited it were not supernatural; and he resolved to explore the mystery, if possible.

The old man gave him a very warm reception, put his mule into an unthatched hovel, which was dignified by the appellation of stable, laid the only leathern cushion he possessed upon the one-armed elbow chair, set before him a jug of goat's milk, a small batch of bread, and a few bunches of grapes, and pressed him to taste them. Altador was in return obliged to gratify his host's curiosity, in regard to all that had passed at the baron's mansion.

Towards noon, Hugo's daughter, a fine strapping girl of nineteen, who earned her daily sustenance in a neighbouring vineyard, returned home to prepare her father's midday repast; and she this day went about it with additional diligence, seeing that a guest of Altador's deportment was to partake of it; and repeatedly did she remind him of the honour he conferred on her father's cottage, who, on his part, commanded her not to mention to any one who was his guest.

Jaquenetta was a hale florid wench, without the slightest dash of prudery in her composition; she used every winning art she was acquainted with, to inspire Altador with as strong a regard for her, as she had at first sight felt for him; but his thoughts were too much occupied by the transactions of the preceding days, to suffer him to pay any attention to her little arts; and after the repast, Jaquenetta was under the necessity of returning to her labour, without the reward of a single smile for her neat meal from Altador, which her fine black eyes had not ceased to challenge.

"Go thy way, Jaquenetta," cried the old man, as she left the cottage; "thou art now my only hope: mayest thou be wiser and happier than thy poor mother, Heaven rest her soul in peace!—She is the very picture of poor Rosala," continued he, turning to Altador, who immediately inquired if he had any particular reason for the wish he had just expressed.

"She was unguarded in her youth," returned the good man, "and that brought sorrow when she came to the age of reflection. Ah! many a one," continued Hugo, "hath been undone by a flattering tongue and proffered purse."

"Was she untrue to thee?" asked the youth.

"No, by the Virgin!" answered Hugo; "after I married her, she was as true to me as faith and love could bind her; but ere that time she was decoyed into a villain's arms, who left her and her infant destitute upon the world. I always had entertained a kindness for her, and I could not bear to see her starving; so I married her, and treated her babe as if it had been my own; it died, poor infant, about a year after, or it might be fifteen months—nay, by my troth, now I recollect myself, 'twas whilst thou were at nurse with Rosala."

73

"That is before my remembrance," cried Altador, smiling at Hugo's ingenuousness.

"She loved thee as dearly as her own," replied Hugo. "Heaven, in its mercy, gave her Jaquenetta, to supply the loss of him it took; had it lived, it should never have known the want of a father. Rosala died a penitent; and she is blest, I make no doubt."

"Didst thou ever learn from her who was the seducer of her virtue?" said Altador.

"No, verily," answered the old man; "she had promised she never would betray him, and though he treated her so cruelly, she kept her word."

With various other tales concerning his own family, interspersed with some anecdotes relating to the former baron, all tending to show his regard for his old master, did Hugo, with the unwearied garulity natural to old age, run on, until his daughter again returned from the vineyard; and he now went to assist her in driving home from a neighbouring mountain, a few goats, which made up the greatest part of his wealth; and Jaquenetta, having milked and enclosed them in the fold, prepared their homely supper, consisting of a few boiled lupines, a cheese made of goat's milk, a cup of new wine, and some fresh-gathered grapes. This meal afforded Jaquenetta much greater satisfaction than the midday repast had done; for Altador, having been informed that she bore the exact resemblance of her deceased mother, wished, he knew not why, to make himself acquainted with her countenance: and thus, to her no small gratification, his eyes frequently encountered hers. She was now going to prepare him a pallet of clean straw, when she heard, with the greatest regret, that he was not to pass the night in the cottage; whither he was going, her father considered it as most prudent to let her remain ignorant, and ordered her to retire to rest. When she, at length, after many forced delays, had ascended the ladder which led to her miserable chamber, the old man, in compliance with Altador's wish immediately to depart, took up his lamp, together with the proper implements for striking a light, and having placed them in an old battered lanthorn, they left the cottage.

Jaquenetta, on hearing them shut the door, could not resist forcing her head out of a chink, which served to admit both air and light into her chamber, and calling out—"Good night," to Altador, who cordially returned her wish, and then proceeded onwards with her father.

When they had walked for the space of some minutes in silence—"Then thou wilt go?" exclaimed the old man.

"I have told thee my resolution," returned Altador.

After a short pause—"I dare not go with thee," said Hugo.

"I wish to be alone," replied the youth.

"Pray the Virgin thou mayest be so," cried the old man, with uplifted hands and eyes.

"Why should I fear the anger of either God or man?" exclaimed Altador; "I have not knowingly offended any man; nor does my conscience upbraid me with any sin towards my God."

"That I will readily believe," answered the old man; "but should evil spirits assail thee?"

"Evil spirits have no power over the righteous," interrupted Altador.

"Then Heaven wots thou wilt be safe," cried the old man, in an ecstacy.

Little more passed till they arrived within a short distance of the castle, when Hugo, having lighted the lamp, and commended him to the care of the Saints, hobbled away as fast as his old limbs could carry him.

Altador now proceeded to the castle, and having entered by the western gate, which he marvelled at again finding open, when the others were so strongly locked, cast a look round the hall, and perceiving that every thing remained in the same situation in which he had left it a few days before, ascended to his father's study, where he meant to pass the night; he examined it attentively—nothing seemed to have been moved from its place; he then closed all the doors leading to the small closet, as well as that which opened upon the gallery; and having drawn one of the best-conditioned chairs to a table which stood in the middle of the apartment, and upon which he placed his lamp and drawn sword, seated himself, and taking from his pocket a book which he had brought with him, to divert, if possible, his thoughts from the gloomy scene around him, began reading. His book contained a history of the famous Charlemagne, and the warmth with which he re-fought the battles of that great hero, in a short time took entire possession of his thoughts. At length his lamp growing dim, he was under the necessity of laying down his book to trim the wick. As he was taking it up, his attention was arrested by a clanking of chains, accompanied by a deep groan, seemingly underneath the apartment in which he was sitting—he listened attentively—after a minute's interval it died away—some time now elapsed, and it did not return. He now began to imagine that his senses had deceived him, so casting a glance over each of the doors, he resumed his subject—he had not turned the page ere the same sounds again struck his ear, but they now seemed to proceed from the small closet which terminated the suite of apartments, in the first of which he now was: he again listened; the groans became much plainer than before, and he distinctly heard the clanking of chains: he again laid down his book; the sound approached towards him—the chains rattled vehemently; scarcely had he sprung from his chair, and seized his sword, ere the door, leading to the suite of rooms, flew open, and a spectre, whose arms and legs were fastened with heavy chains, with a naked body covered with wounds, from which the blood still seemed to gush, with clotted hair and eyes dripping with blood, rendered visible by a flame which burnt on the crown of its head, replete with purple gashes, stood before him, and uttered three deep groans. Altador, summoning all the courage he was master of, exclaimed—"What wouldst thou with me?" The figure pointed to the outward door. "Who art thou?" cried Altador. The spectre shook its head, heaved a sigh, and again pointed to the door. "Speak, what art thou?" repeated Altador. The spectre again pointed to the door, making a sign for him to go out, and giving him to understand that it would follow him: upon this, Altador opened the door—the figure advanced to the middle of the apartment, Altador still retreating with his sword pointed towards it: he had now passed the threshold—the spectre again followed him, and pointed to the stairs—Altador turned his eyes towards them, and in an instant the figure vanished, and the door was closed with a loud crash.

Altador, on the spectre's pointing to him to leave the apartment, had fortunately taken up his lamp; and thus, happily for him, amidst his present terrors, he was not left in total darkness, which would, in no small degree, have added to his alarm. On somewhat recovering his courage, which had met with no inconsiderable shock, he resolved, if possible, to open the door with his sword, as he once before had done, and endeavour to find what course the figure had taken. No sooner had he begun this operation, than he heard a loud and dismal groan—he listened a moment, but steeling himself against all fear, he proceeded to make a second cut. A hollow voice now exclaimed—"Forbear!" This somewhat staggered him; but he determined to make one more attempt, and for this purpose set down his lamp, that he might be the better able to effect his design. The same voice now cried— "Fly from hence, and avoid thy destruction." At the same instant, he heard all the doors in the suite of apartments, shut violently one after another, whilst he stood rapt in astonishment: what had not before occurred to him darted across his mind—that the lock, which he had a few evenings before cut out with his sword, had been replaced; this convinced him that some mortals had been in the castle; but whether the inhabitants were so or not, he was at a loss to determine.

Not knowing how to proceed under these alarming circumstances, he determined to go down into the hall, and take a more accurate view of it than he had yet done; he could not help supposing that there necessarily must be some apartments under the four galleries, which formed the angles of the castle. Having descended, he held his lamp close to the walls in many parts, but could perceive nothing except niches and carvings in the wainscot, that seemed to have been designed as ornaments. He now conjectured that there might be passages in what the baron called the kitchen, leading to those apartments—if there were any such, and he accordingly resolved to explore it: having entered and surveyed it, without being able to discover a single mark of any outlet, he was upon the point of re-entering the hall, when the distant clanking of chains again struck his ear; he stopped to listen—he heard the noise distinctly under him for some minutes, in the same manner as he had done in the upper apartment—a clash now followed, as it were of all the chains falling together to the earth—all was now again silent.

During the time that he had been hearkening to this noise, a large old closet in one corner of the kitchen, the doors of which were thrown carelessly together, caught his eye; he opened them, and a putrid stench immediately flew up his nostrils, but he could not imagine whence it proceeded; he applied his lamp to the wainscot, and perceived a rusty ring, seemingly of brass, fixed in the wall; he pulled at it, and by a slight effort, it followed his hand, carrying along with it part of a decayed panel, and presented to his view the carcase of a man in a state of putrefaction. The sight petrified him, his heart's blood thrilled within him, and ready to sink, he leaned against the side of the closet: horrid as the object was, he could not turn his eyes from it—he gazed upon it in speechless astonishment, when a long and deep sigh met his ear; he started and looked about him, but so small a flame did his lamp throw out, that he seemed to stand in almost impenetrable darkness: he now closed the panel as well as he was able; scarcely had he effected it, ere another sigh passed by him; instantly he shut the closet doors, and with big drops of perspiration standing on his face, he left the kitchen, closing the doors cautiously after him.

"Who may not that corpse have been?" was the first thought that entered the distracted brain of the fainting Altador, as he leaned against a broken pillar in the hall. "Who may not that corpse have been?"—but he drove away all reflections tending to it, unable to bear them in his present situation: he wished to leave the castle, but whither could he go?—from his uncle's he had been driven, on a bare suspicion of that, which, had it been so, he should have gloried in avowing. He cursed the unhappy chance that led them both to the same spot—doubly he cursed it, as that interview had made him so fully acquainted with what he had long feared to inquire into; and the mystery in which Matilda had clouded her declaration, had added not a little to aggravate the distress of his mind; he mourned that he could no longer impart his sorrows to the tender Hypolita, and profit by her counsel; he longed, but he knew not how, to see her.

Whether he should return instantly to Hugo's cottage, and fly this alarming scene, was his next consideration; prudence forbade him so to do, by reminding him, that his return before the morning, would, without doubt, fire all the old man's superstitious fears, which had already been powerfully excited, and probably, by means of his daughter's prattling, create an alarm in the neighbourhood, which might discover to the baron, that he had not, in compliance with his orders, immediately proceeded to the monastery. At length, after much deliberation, he resolved to remain where he now was till day began to dawn, and then to go in search of his mule, and, without delay, set out towards Cordova.

Whilst wrapt in similar reflections, his attention was suddenly excited by the creaking of a door upon its hinges, seemingly near to where he stood; in less than a minute's interval, he perceived a panel in the wainscot of the hall drawn up, and a man's legs appearing under it; upon this, he held the skirts of his mantle before his lamp, to prevent his being discovered by the light of it: the person now stepped cautiously out, let the panel drop, and proceeded to the eastern gate; having unlocked it, he went out, and Altador heard the door locked after him. He was now certain that *some* of the inhabitants of this castle were human beings; and he much doubted whether even the figure he had seen was not some one in disguise, placed there to terrify those who visited the castle by night, but on what account, he could not form the most distant idea.

This conjecture gave him fresh courage, and he again ascended into the northern gallery, resolving to hazard one more attempt towards the discovery he so earnestly desired to make: he found the door still locked; he knocked loudly; no answer was returned. Upon this, he determined once more to apply his sword to the lock; this effort succeeded, and he was again within the haunted apartment: his book was still lying on the table as he had left it. He now proceeded to the other apartments, and lastly arrived in the closet; here was to be his particular search, in order to find by what means the spectre had effected its escape.

The words of his uncle now again recurred to his recollection, and he shuddered at the thought: he examined the closet with the most minute scrutiny; he lifted up the tapestry, and tried every panel beneath it; they were all immoveable: as he stood with his eyes fixed on the floor, which he was now exploring with the greatest minuteness, his attention was drawn to a small shining knob in one of the boards; he touched it with his sword; it gave way; he now pushed at it harder than before—it slid from him—instantly he felt himself slipping through a trap door, which shut with a snap, and left him in total darkness, as the current of air, which met him in his descent, had extinguished his lamp.

CHAPTER III

Good shepherd, tell this youth what 'tis to love.
It is to be made all of sighs and tears;
It is to be made all of faith and service;
It is to be made all of phantasy;
All made of passion, and all made of wishes,
All adoration, duty, and observance;
All humbleness, all patience, and impatience;
All purity, all trial, all observance.

As You Like It.

MATILDA, on the evening of the day on which the second tournament had been held, on retiring to her apartment, was, as usual, accompanied by Villetta, who, looking full in her mistress's face, exclaimed—"Ah! my lady, it is a good thing for them that have good spirits."

"I know no greater blessing," answered Matilda.

"Then I am sure you are happy, my lady," cried Villetta. "Why, I declare I don't think you have cried at all, for all your husband that was to have been is almost killed. I am sure I should have cried enough, if any such-like thing had happened to Lopez; I told him so just now, my lady, as I met him in the hall; he had just been into the stable to look after his mule—it is not his *own,* my lady, only he calls it so, because he always rides on it, when he goes to Toledo; it is a dark brown colour, my lady; as sleek as a mouse, and as gentle———"

"Reach me a chair," said Matilda, who paid little attention to what Villetta said.

"Oh, the Virgin!—are you faint my lady?"

"Not at all," answered Matilda, "only somewhat weary; I have walked a good deal during the course of the day."

"To be sure, my lady, you did not look as if you were faint; your cheeks are just like two roses; but I thought it would not have been much of a wonder if you had. Oh, holy Maria! if the duke should die, what a sad thing it would be, would it not, my lady?—should not you be greatly grieved, my lady?"

"I should commiserate the fate of any one who had been cut off, without due time for repentance," returned Matilda.

"Dear, my lady," cried Villetta, "sure you can't suppose that such a fine, handsome, good-looking, rich, noble, valiant gentleman as the duke, and that was to have been your husband and all, can have any sins to repent of—has he, my lady? Did you ever hear of any murder he committed, or any thing bad, my lady?"

Matilda, who now found that she had been unguarded in her expression, answered—"Never; I only meant that the best of us need repentance, though the good in a smaller degree than the more wicked; and I felt pity for those who have deferred it to the last moments of their existence."

"Ah, my lady! it is a terrible thing not to repent of one's sins before one dies, and to have one's ghost walk and howl about of a night."

"I believe, Villetta," returned Matilda, "your head runs on little else besides ghosts; how can you be so foolish?"

"Well, my lady, it is well for poor spirits that every body is not so misbelieving as you are, and don't make such a joke of them, or they would find nobody to make confession to, when they had been walking, night after night, on purpose."

"If it were possible," replied Matilda, "which I firmly believe it is not, for the dead to rise again in this world, your timorous disposition would not be much more friendly to them than mine, I think."

"Oh! but, my lady, one can't help seeing them, if one is ever so much afraid of them: why, old Roberto, my uncle, saw his wife's ghost, you know, my lady, and it spoke to him, and he is as much afraid of a spirit as I am; did I never tell you the story about it, my lady?"

"No."

"Well, my lady, I am surprised at that; it was about six years ago, on Christmas eve—it spoiled our Christmas frolic, I am sure, we were all so frightened; my uncle had roast pork for dinner that day, I well remember, but I could not eat much for thinking of the ghost; should not you like to hear about it, my lady?"

"I shall be a very incredulous hearer, and therefore, not at all one to your mind, I dare say," returned Matilda.

"Well, pray let me tell you, my lady," cried Villetta; "I did not promise any body I would not tell it; I did not indeed, my lady; it is not a secret."

"That I readily believe, since you are intrusted with it," said Matilda.

"Nay, my lady, pray don't jeer me; you know I did not tell the secret at last; and it was well I did not, for Jerome said to me the next night, 'Villetta,' said he—we were talking about his having been to the castle with my lord, to look for the spirit; and now I think of it, my lady, I must tell you, that I don't believe the ghost does live at the castle; for though it mayn't walk in the daytime, yet they must have found it, had it been there—for where could it have hid itself? Well, 'Villetta,' says he, 'have you been prattling to-day about who I said I thought the spirit was?' 'No, by the holy saints!' cried I, 'I have not;' and as I knew I had not, I felt as happy—"

"As the recollection of having acted rightly can never fail to render you," interrupted Matilda.

"Ay, it was very well as it was, to be sure, my lady:—well, about my aunt's ghost, I must tell you that; so, as I was saying, it was Christmas eve, and my uncle was gone to bed; he slept in a little room all alone; and when he was just asleep——Was not that a noise, my lady?"

"No, no."

"Are you sure of it, my lady?"

"To be sure I am; it is only your flurried imagination; come, come, leave off telling these stories, and go to your own bed."

"No, indeed I must finish it, my lady;—so, when he was just asleep, he thought he heard his door open, and he looked out of bed, and he saw a woman all in white, and she said to him in a hollow voice,"——At that instant a voice, similar to the one Villetta was describing, pronounced Matilda's name.

Villetta shrieked aloud; Matilda chid her for her foolish apprehensions, and bade her open the door. At the idea of seeing a ghost, as she imagined that the voice could not proceed from any one save a spirit, she hesitated to comply with her mistress's order; and Matilda, seeing her fear of doing as she had commanded her, rose, and opened the door herself: she was somewhat startled on looking into the gallery, as she perceived there was no one near, and was just going to communicate her alarm to Villetta, who had remained fixed in the place where she had been standing to assist Matilda in undressing, when she again heard her name mentioned.

Villetta now exclaimed—"Oh! my lady, it is somebody on the green that is calling to you; do, my lady, open the window, and see who it is."

Matilda approached towards the casement, and listened; a third repetition of the same word confirmed her in Villetta's opinion, and she raised the window: looking down, she beheld a man, mounted on a mule, who, on seeing her, exclaimed—"Dearest love, 'tis I." It was the well known voice of the young peasant that addressed her. Ere she could reply, he continued—"Swiftly, I beseech thee, let down somewhat, to which I may fasten this paper; dearest Matilda, be quick and silent."

Matilda instantly tore the ribband from her head-dress, and tying it to that which she had just taken from her waist, dropped one end from the window, holding the other end in her hands. The young peasant, vaulting from his mule, instantly fastened a letter to the extremity of the ribband, and exclaimed—"On thy compliance with this request, depends my future happiness or misery; farewell!" So saying, he jumped upon his mule, and was almost immediately hid from her sight by the gloominess of the night.

In a transport of joy, impatience, and astonishment, she flew towards the lamp on the table, close by which stood the still more astonished Villetta, whom, till that moment, Matilda had entirely forgotten to be in the chamber, and who now cried—"Ah, my lady! I thought you had something to keep up your spirits for the loss of the duke."

Matilda was unable to speak with vexation at the idea of what she had so cautiously concealed from every one, being now made known to a girl of Villetta's tattling disposition: Villetta perceived her confusion, and exclaimed—"Now, my lady, I'll shew you I can keep a secret; for by the Holy Mother of God, I'll never tell any body of that letter."

"Hush, hush," said Matilda, "I require no such solemn asseverations; your word would have been sufficient, as I hope you are incapable of betraying one, for whom you have always shewn so great an affection."

"Oh! my lady, the Holy Virgin knows I do not love any body so well as you; I don't love Lopez quite so well as you, my lady; and I am sure I always had such a respect for lord Altador, that I would not betray him for a hundred pistoles."

"You are much mistaken," returned Matilda, "if you suppose the person who spoke to me under the window to be Altador."

"Dear my lady, well, I am sure I thought it had, you always seemed to like him so vastly well: who was it then, my lady? may I not know? indeed and indeed you may trust me—I won't blab—I have sworn I won't."

"Lock the door," said Matilda, who knew not what answer to make to Villetta's last inquiry: "I must read this paper before I can tell you any thing more."

She now broke the seal and read as follows:—

"DEAREST LADY,

The deceitful duke of Gonsalez, who is in reality but slightly wounded by the unknown knight, feigneth a most severe indisposition, which simulation he trusteth will forward a design he has formed against the peace of my beloved Matilda, whom he well knoweth to detest him: the only method by which she can insure herself against the impending danger, is to seek that asylum which has before been offered her, by him, who now repeats those vows of constancy which he has already made in her beloved presence, and to which he adheres not with less firmness in her absence, her loved idea being always present to his thoughts. If she will essay once more to meet him in the evening of the morrow, at the hour of eleven, in that fatal grove, where, three nights since, cursing the perversity of the fates, he sought her, alas! in vain, he will convey her to a place of safety; where, if she will condescend to share his fortunes, the good father Anselm (thou marvellest at these words, but I cannot now explain them) shall connect us by the bonds of love inseparable. If thou hast, dearest lady, any female, faithful to thy interest, whom thou canst safely trust, I will afford her also an asylum together with thee, that thou mayest enjoy the society of one of thine own sex. Deign, my Matilda, to fly from base ingratitude and cruelty, to him whose love makes every labour, every danger undergone for thee, delight: fly to the protection of him who liveth but in thee—thy ever faithful, ever constant

HENRICO."

Matilda, having perused the foregoing lines, heaved a deep sigh, upon which Villetta exclaimed—"Oh! my dear lady, what is the matter?"

Matilda, regardless of Villetta's inquiry, now cried aloud— "Oh, cruel father! unfortunate Matilda!"

"How are you unfortunate, my dear lady? can I do any thing to serve you? I pity you very much, indeed I do, my lady. Ah! I guess how it is; you want to marry some nice young lord, rather than the old duke. I see how it is, my lady; I should not like an old man myself—no, not even if he was covered with diamonds. Ay, marriage for money seldom ends happily; my poor cousin Bertha hanged herself for vexation, after she had married an old man for his riches; and he was not so old as the duke, my lady; I do suppose her ghost walked and upbraided him, my lady; but that, I never could hear. And so, the baron won't let you have the man of your heart, my lady? Well, if I had such a cross father——"

"What would'st thou do, Villetta?" interrupted Matilda.

"Why, I say, my lady, if you loved him now so very much, as I love Lopez, and he loves me, and we are very fond of one another, we are indeed, my lady—we are booksworn by an oath, and that you know is a very sacred thing, my lady—I'd play him such a trick."

"Wouldst thou marry without his consent?" asked Matilda.

"Not exactly so, my lady; but I'd run away from him; and then, if he did not fetch me back, and seem very anxious about me, my lady—why, as I could not live quite all alone, why, I'd e'en marry the man I liked, and live with him, my lady."

Matilda could not help smiling at the artless manner in which Villetta had related her little plot; and having again enjoined her to secrecy, which Villetta again solemnly promised to observe, she proceeded to inform her how she was circumstanced, and her intention of making one more attempt on the following night to escape from her father's mansion. Villetta having expressed her unfeigned astonishment at the discovery which her lady had made to her, Matilda imparted to her the contents of the letter; and lastly asked her, whether she would be that faithful female.

Villetta, for a moment, during which her eyes seemed to say—must I leave Lopez behind?—hesitated to answer; but the momentary struggle being past, she replied—"I would follow you any where, my lady; and yet, my lady," stifling her tears and sobbing, "I am going to *leave* Lopez behind, and you are going to *meet* your faithful Henrico; I should be so very happy, my lady, if Lopez might go."

"It must not be," returned Matilda, with an air of authority she was unwont to assume, hoping thus to check in its rise a latent wish, which she imagined she saw ready to burst from Villetta's lips, of informing Lopez of their intended departure, and which she feared might lead to a discovery of her elopement, ere she was beyond the reach of those whose resentment she so strongly dreaded. "It must not be; it may appear to you, Villetta, a hardship, that when I myself am going to the man, whom of all others I hold most dear, I should wish to tear you from *him* who possesses *your* affections; but weigh the matter well in your own breast, and you will perceive that our cases are widely different; you will then, I think, freely own, that your desire of taking Lopez along with you, proceeds but too much from an idle wish to gratify your vanity, and that I am flying from a cruel and unrelenting father, to one who will afford me his protection as a friend, rather than as a husband."

Villetta was too sensible of the truth of Matilda's words to venture to make any contradictory reply; and in a very short time became reconciled to parting with Lopez, consoling herself either with the idea of soon beholding him again, or perhaps the more flattering one of making some new conquest; for Villetta, though she had nothing more to boast of than a clear skin and ruddy cheeks, was by no means destitute of that vanity, which, in every rank of life, attaches itself indiscriminately to the softer sex.

After innumerable questions on the part of Villetta, as to, "Who the young peasant might prove to be?—Where might be the place of his abode?—Whether he lived alone?—Whether he inhabited a castle?—Whether his mansion stood at a great distance from the baron's seat?—How he could possibly know any thing about the duke and poor father Anselm?—And whether, perchance he might have so good a looking servant as Lopez?" to which Matilda could give but very unsatisfactory answers, they retired to Matilda's bed, who thought it most advisable to keep Villetta as much as possible in her sight.

CHAPTER IV

Mildly beam'd the queen of night,
　　Sailing thro' the grey serene;
Silver'd by her modest light,
　　But faintly shone the solitary scene,
With deep'ning shadows mixt, and glitt'ring breaks between.
Silent was all around,
　　Save where the swelling breeze,
Convey'd the half expiring sound
　　Of distant water-falls and gently waving trees.

PENROSE.

MATILDA arose at an early hour, and having once more collected such valuables as she possessed, she formed them, together with a few necessaries, into a small packet, and carefully deposited them underneath the bed.

Villetta, who seemed entirely to have forgotten not less her last night's sorrow than the occasion of it, testified the greatest joy at her approaching journey, and was delighted with the idea of going she knew not whither, nor with whom.

Matilda almost feared to see the lady Hypolita, lest her looks should betray the feelings of her heart; and accordingly invented the most plausible excuses her wandering thoughts would allow her to frame, for remaining the greatest part of the day alone in her chamber, or at least, accompanied by Villetta only.

During supper, information was brought the baron, that the duke of Gonsalez was much mended, and requested to see him on the following morning. Garcia, on receipt of this message, cast a look of sullen joy at his daughter, which bespoke a soul exulting in the completion of its plans, however agonizing to those whose welfare it is its first obligation to consult. The colour retiring from Matilda's cheeks, plainly disclosed the emotions of her heart, stung by her father's remorseless conduct. The lady Hypolita participated in her sorrow; she would have spoken to her, and endeavoured to have comforted her, but the baron's fiery eye at that moment meeting hers, overawed her from giving utterance to the consolatory words with which she was about to address Matilda; she hung down her head, and dropped a tear in silence.

How mournful were the reflections of the unhappy Matilda, when once more alone! how did she bewail the sudden and un-provoked storm, which had clouded the sunshine of her early days, and at length drove her to seek protection in the arms of a stranger, against the cruelty of an obdurate father! Happily her meditations were not of long duration; Villetta almost immediately roused her by this exclamation—"Dear my lady, won't you take Luco along with you?"

"Certainly not," answered Matilda; "I shall take no unnecessary incumbrance."

"Nay, my lady, I did not know but you might like him to defend you: don't you take any thing then, my lady?"

"That small packet," replied Matilda, "contains all I want."

"Oh! well, my lady, I have put all my money, and all the linen I want, into my pocket, and I am sure while they last, my poor dear lady shan't want."

This affectionate declaration drew a tear from Matilda; and her bosom glowed with gratitude, towards one who was still true to her amidst all her calamities.

After a few minutes silence, Villetta cried—"I fancy every body is in bed, my lady."

"Open the door softly and listen," said Matilda.

"Yes, my lady; all is quite still," replied Villetta.

"Let us then depart," returned Matilda; "the clock at the monastery now strikes eleven."

With slow steps and the greatest caution, they arrived in the hall; Matilda carefully unbarred the door—Villetta trembled from head to foot, and yet affected to wear a smile of the greatest satisfaction and security. They were now on the green before the mansion; the moon gave a dim light, scarcely sufficient to guard them against the stones and roots of trees that were scattered in various parts. They stopped and listened; a dead silence prevailed—"Are you sure it was to-night, my lady?" asked Villetta, after they had waited for about a quarter of an hour.

"Hark! I now hear the trampling of mules," exclaimed Matilda.

"Oh! there they are, there they come!" cried Villetta, in an ecstacy; "let us go and meet them, my lady." So saying, she advanced without waiting for Matilda's permission. The persons now rode up to them, when a rough voice exclaimed—"Ah! my lasses, what, not yet in bed? ye keep late hours at the baron's."

What were the sensations of Matilda, when she heard these words uttered by a voice, which she instantly recollected to be that of one of the duke of Gonsalez's esquires; however, she had sufficient presence of mind to answer—"No such good luck for us, gentlemen, as to reside at the baron's; my sister and I are going home to the neighbouring village. Good night, good gentlemen." So saying, she caught hold of Villetta's arm, and they proceeded forward. One of the men having said something which Matilda did not understand, they all burst into a loud laugh, clapped spurs to their mules, and galloped towards the baron's mansion.

"Oh! the Virgin, what an escape, my lady! I am sure I trembled enough, did not you, my lady?"

"For Heaven's sake, proceed as fast as you are able," returned Matilda, regardless of her prattling companion's inquiries, and scarcely able to breathe through fear.

"But whither are you going, my lady?" rejoined Villetta; "we ought to have waited near the mansion for lord Henrico; if we should miss him now, my lady?"

"This is the road he took last night," said Matilda; "at all events, we must on no account approach the mansion while those men are so near; so come along, Villetta."

They had not proceeded many steps, ere, to their inexpressible joy, the young peasant came running towards them; and now, Matilda, actuated by the delight of the moment, congratulated herself on having escaped every danger. Alas! how little did she foresee the calamities that awaited her!

Henrico, seizing her hand, and imprinting on it a fervent kiss, informed her in a low voice, that his companion, the elder peasant, was stationed at a short distance in waiting for them, and entreated them to make what haste they were able towards his mules, as they had every thing to fear whilst they remained within sight of the mansion—"This night," continued he, "the unfeeling baron had appointed to surrender thee unto the crafty duke."

"Oh, gracious God!" cried Matilda, in a transport of grief, "we shall be pursued; I but now parted with the duke's esquire; happily for me, he did not then recognise me. Let us quicken our steps, I beseech you."

Having at length reached the mules, the young peasant placed Villetta before his companion, and taking up Matilda before himself, they proceeded as swiftly as the darkness of the night would permit them, for the moon was now entirely hidden from their sight, partly by the thick clouds which were continually passing over its surface, and partly by the gloomy shade of the intervening trees through which they were journeying.

They had not proceeded far, ere the sound of mules in full speed arrested their attention. Henrico and his friend spurred on their beasts, and encouraged their fair companions, whose hearts were beginning greatly to sink. They now swept down the declivity of a hill; an instantaneous stop at the bottom, during which they heard no sounds, somewhat abated their alarm, but by no means their speed: a short but steep ascent now obliged them to retard their pace, and they again heard their pursuers, seemingly much nearer than before. Matilda seized the arm of Henrico, and with difficulty kept herself from fainting. Villetta, who had not hitherto mustered sufficient courage to address one to whom she was an utter stranger, now began to find her tongue, and gave free vent to her fears in unfeigned accents of terror, delivered in so elevated a tone, that her companion did not cease entreating her to lower her voice, lest it should be the means of discovering them.

The mules now approached nearer, voices were distinctly heard; Matilda uttered a feeble shriek, and sunk upon Henrico; he still spurred on his mule, and called to his friend Alphonso to do the same by his; but the overburthened animals, panting with fatigue and loss of breath, were at length obliged involuntarily to slacken their steps, regardless of the galling steel.

Their pursuers, who were the same men that had addressed Matilda and Villetta, and who, as it had been preconcerted by the baron Garcia and the duke of Gonsalez, were during the course of the night to have carried Matilda from her father's mansion to that of the duke, arriving at the baron's, and finding her not there, had immediately set out in pursuit of her; and having, unfortunately for her, followed the track she had taken, now rode up, and having rushed upon Henrico and Alphonso, notwithstanding their brave endeavours to defend themselves, seized, gagged, and bound them: resistance was in vain opposed to so superior a force; the vassals of the duke were twelve in number, headed by his esquire, Manfred; Matilda was placed, almost lifeless, on a mule before him—Villetta before one of the vassals, to whom she afforded no small entertainment by her screams, repeated entreaties for freedom, and exaggeration of the presents which she said her mistress would heap on them, provided they released her and lord Henrico.

The desponding lover and his friend were fixed on their own beasts, under whose bodies the ruffians bound their legs, having first confined their arms. Words cannot describe the sensations of Henrico; they can be pictured only in those susceptible breasts which can feel for his situation, and pity it: a sigh of rage, the first sentiment of his heart, on finding his hopes thus cruelly defeated, and himself in ignominious bondage, burst from his swollen bosom; a groan of bitter anguish, occasioned by the hard fate of his beloved Matilda, quickly succeeded it. Who could bear to have the cup dashed from his hand, ere he had yet moistened his parched lips? Who could tamely bear to have toiled over the quicksands of doubt into the flowery path of happiness, and ere he had proceeded a single step, sink into the abyss of despair? To be a captive—in bonds—ignorant of his fate, and sensible only to the tortures of mind which Matilda on the return of her senses would feel for him—the thought was agony: at that instant he heard her murmur his name; his ardent wish to relieve her anxiety gave him strength, and in the madness of the moment, he split the gag—"I am here, dearest love," he exclaimed.

"Would to God thou wert not!" cried Matilda; "if I must submit to the base tyrant's will, why have the cruel fates ordained that thou must suffer with me?"

"His freedom will be granted, on your compliance with the duke's will," said Manfred.

"That," exclaimed the half-frantic Henrico, for that moment forgetting his own situation, "shall never be whilst I can wield a sword."

"But there are ways to prevent thee, young braggart," returned the esquire.

"And there is a power," replied the youth, "to avenge the cause of wronged innocence."

"Nay, nay," cried Manfred, "reserve that language for the duke; I have but obeyed him in what I have done, and you know, not less than I, that it is my business to obey his orders."

"To commit injustice," replied Henrico, "can be the business of no man: ask your conscience whether it can justify your proceeding towards us."

"Conscience!" repeated Manfred, and a loud laugh from the rest of the vassals plainly indicated to the forlorn Henrico that remonstrances were in vain.

At length they arrived in silence at the duke's castle; Manfred, the esquire, hailed the porters to let down the drawbridge; an immediate answer was returned, and the heavy bridge flapped loudly down; they then passed over the moat, and entered the castle gates. The lights which shone from several windows of the castle, indistinctly shewed them many men in arms scattered about the court-yard: they also heard a confused noise of talking, but could not distinguish what was said; the gates were now shut, and the weighty chains by which the portcullis was suspended, opposed a horrid clanking to the silence of the midnight hour.

Not less to enjoy his triumph in the midst of splendour, than to display the charms of his fair mistress, Gaspero had assembled at a board of festivity, all the companions of his profligate hours, and instruments of his absolute will; amongst these were several females, some of whom he had raised to their present delusive and unhappy situation, at the price of their virtue; others had been betrayed into his arms, by the abettors of his crimes.

Since his overthrow by the unknown knight, not a single smile of satisfaction had beamed on his fierce brow until this night, when the thought of possessing her, whom for the present moment he considered as the only woman on earth worthy of his regard, had elevated him to a pitch of ecstacy little inferior to madness. His obedient companions were constrained to assimilate that joy in which they participated not; wine had been called in, to aid in rousing their spirits; and the whole castle rang with their clamorous shouts and laughter: heated by drink, their mirth became licentious, and the doors of the marble hall being thrown open, presented to Matilda a scene she wanted faith to believe really passing before her eyes.

The duke instantly sprang from his seat, and was advancing towards Matilda, when he suddenly stopped, and casting his eyes on Henrico and Alphonso, asked who those prisoners were?

"Most noble duke," exclaimed the fawning esquire, Manfred, "thus may every one that dares to be thy foe, fall within thy power. Behold, in this man, a pretender to the love of the lady Matilda; on this very night he had seduced her from her father, the baron of Ollada's mansion, and was conveying her beyond his reach, when we most fortunately overtook and bound him."

"Thanks, my more than saviour—my best of friends!—this gallant deed shall not go unrewarded," cried Gaspero. "As for this presumptuous wretch, my sword shall quickly end his daring spirit."

So saying, he rushed towards Henrico, who had, till this moment, stood with his face concealed in his mantle, but now falling on his knee, and presenting his breast, exclaimed—"Strike, I am ready to receive the blow!"

"Hell and demons!" cried the duke, and sunk into the arms of his attendants.

Matilda flew to Henrico, and fainted on his neck: the revellers immediately rose from the banquet, and in great consternation, flocked round the duke. In a minute's interval he opened his eyes with these words—"Away, and give me air!" They accordingly retired from before him, and left open to his view Henrico, who was supporting the fainting Matilda:—"'Tis he, 'tis he," instantly continued the duke, while the swelling drops of perspiration burst from every muscle, and his knees shook beneath his trembling frame. "See, he protects *her* and mocks *me!*—Strike at me with thy keenest reproaches, I merit them all: Oh! torture, torture! Thou hast once been merciful, and I have abused thy goodness! Oh! do not crush me! say thou wilt spare me—Oh! spare me, spare me!" and again sunk lifeless into the arms of his attendants, whom Manfred ordered to carry him to his own chamber, whilst Henrico and Alphonso were, by his commands, dragged from the sinking Matilda, and thrown into a dungeon in a remote part of the castle.

True and faithful friends suffering under the same misfortunes, and unable to afford each other the slightest consolation, rather than wound the ears of those they love with vain lamentations, sigh away the melancholy hours in silence. Thus it was with Henrico and Alphonso; no sound, save the clock on the loftiest tower of the castle, which had just proclaimed the first hour of the succeeding day, had interrupted the sad stillness of their gloomy prison, when the rusty bolts moving in their sockets, and the heavy door creaking upon its hinges, presented to their sight Estifania, the favourite paramour of the duke of Gonsalez.

CHAPTER V

——Frailty, thy name is woman.

Hamlet.

ESTIFANIA, who on the arrival of Henrico and Matilda in the festive hall, was reclining her head on the bosom of Gaspero, had been stabbed to the heart, by the seemingly great rapture with which he welcomed his intended duchess, and from the moment she perceived the dazzling beauty of her rival, silently vowed revenge against both her and the duke: she cast her envious eyes on Matilda, and wished them basilisks to have struck her dead on the instant. But with far other feelings did she behold Henrico; the manly beauty and elegant deportment of the captive youth rivetted her eyes, and through their medium, lighted up a flame in her heart, which speedily diffused itself through her entire frame.

On the first moment that presented itself, she sought Manfred, whom her liberal presents had bound firmly to her interest, and inquired of him who the youth was that had so greatly charmed her.

"Who he is," replied Manfred, "I know not, but I believe him to be of no mean rank; my conjecture is, that he has, on some account unknown to me, assumed the disguise he wears; my reason for this supposition is, that I cannot think the daughter of the haughty baron of Ollada would stoop to the addresses of a peasant youth."

"Surely," interrupted Estifania, "the disguise cannot be assumed for her sake only."

"She has beauties that might warm a heart of ice," returned Manfred; "I tremble when I think of their effect upon the duke."

"They never can have charms for him," cried Estifania; "coldness chills her breast, and her averted eye, sparkling with disdain, will check the rising flame of his desires."

"'Twill fan the flame, I fear," said Manfred; "her haughty coyness will increase the duke's already heated passion. Didst thou not observe how the sight of a rival whom e'en he knows to be within his power, stung him to the soul?"

"Devoid of penetration," exclaimed Estifania, "couldst thou not perceive that some other cause, more weighty than a rival set before his sight, produced the violent agitation with which his every limb was shaken, and called from his lips those incoherent words he uttered?"

"Believe me, lady, my thoughts were in strict unison with thine," replied Manfred, "but at the cause, I cannot guess."

"If the mystery can be fathomed, I will fathom it. Manfred, I love the youth—to madness love him: I am resolved this night to visit him in his dungeon; when there, I will call in, to work therewith upon his heart, every art the cunning of my sex ere practised; if he is formed of mortal composition, I will light the flame of love within his breast; that done, an explanation of the mysteries in which this night's occurrences are clouded, shall be the price I will fix upon the summit of his wishes; that grant once made, no woman ever failed to compass every wish she aimed at; nay, do not knit thy brow, and tell me, as I see thou art prepared to do, of all the trivial dangers unto which I shall expose myself. What most I have to fear, is a discovery by the duke; but should it so fall out, fear not for me; I trust invention will not fail to stand my friend; but lest the youth betrays me, see thou, I care not by what means, prevent his babbling: take this ring—a pledge of secrecy between us. Now give me thy lamp and sword."

"Shall I accompany thee to the prison gate?" asked Manfred.

"On no account," returned Estifania; "get thee to bed; but I charge thee, sleep not, be upon the watch."

"I shall obey you; success attend your enterprise."

"Remember, I can reward those who are faithful to me," said Estifania. So saying, she took the sword and the lamp, and proceeded towards the prison.

Having unbarred the door, she entered, and spoke thus—"I fear I interrupt thy slumbers, gentle stranger."

"No, lady," replied Henrico; "the heart loaded with anguish cannot taste repose. But who art thou that condescendest kindly thus to visit the dreary abode of wretchedness?"

"One that pities thy calamities, and would relieve them."

"Heaven, lady, will reward your generous charity, to a man so wronged, so basely injured, as the wretch who now addresses you. But, oh! lady, my own sufferings are light in comparison to the pangs I feel for her who shares in my unhappy fate."

"Noble youth," returned the insinuating Estifania, "I could almost wish to be in such affliction, that thou mightest pity me; wouldst thou pity me, youth?"

"The unfortunate ever have my commiserations, lady; but thy kinder stars have placed thee happily beyond the bitter gripe of misfortune; thy placid countenance bespeaks a heart at ease within."

"Falsely then does it interpret the feelings of my breast," returned Estifania; "I too have griefs, which thy pity would much alleviate. Why frown you, gentle youth? am I in fault for loving you? No—blame the powers that gave you beauty so transcendent o'er your sex, and that made me but too sensible of its power."

"Shame!" cried Alphonso; "curb thy licentious tongue; art thou a woman, and canst thus debase thy nature?"

"I am a mortal, sir," returned Estifania, "and burn with the desires of one; I do not wish to boast that god-like temperance on which thou, the slave of enervated age, mayest pride thyself; thy frozen blood, now shivering in the winter of old age, disdains to give a thought unto that summer's heat in which thou also once has scorched. If love is a crime, how is the haughty fair you patronize less culpable than I? Is it because her pitying angels have inspired him to return her love, or that she gilds it with the name of virtuous attachment? dress it in whatever garb you will, call it by whatsoever name you please, it is still the impulse of a heart unable to coerce the unruly tide of passion."

"If thou so plainly canst discern the cause productive of this failing in another," interrupted Alphonso, "learn well to temper thine own inclinations, lest, grown absolute, they conspire to thine undoing."

"Thanks for thy caution, old man," cried the hardened Estifania, with a smile of disdain painted on her brow; "I trust I stand upon a base so firm, it cannot easily be shaken. The duke, once satiate of his novel love, will eagerly return to my embraces with increased delight; thus have I ever found him constant in the main, whatever dazzling charms may for a time have drawn him from me."

"And is this," exclaimed Henrico, "all the consolation thou canst offer me, that when a hated rival has plucked off the bud I hold most precious, the withered plant will then, perchance, be mine? Wretched, wretched Henrico!"

"Do not despair, but hear me," answered Estifania. "Unless thou follow my instructions with the most scrupulous exactness, to-morrow's sun will see the baron of Ollada's daughter duchess of Gonsalez. By the assistance of the esquire Manfred I now came hither; I tell thee this, that thou mayest know who are my friends: but, ere I proceed in my attempt at serving thee, there is one circumstance with which it is necessary I should be made acquainted; thou must inform me, why, at the sight of thee, the duke appeared in such alarm; nay, do not hesitate to answer me; tell me but that, I conjure thee, and I am only and entirely thine: without that knowledge, all my efforts in thy behalf will be in vain."

Henrico now cast a significant glance at his friend, and spoke thus—"If I gratify thy excited curiosity, wilt thou promise me inviolable secrecy?"

"Inspire my tongue, ye blessed angels," exclaimed Estifania, raising her impious hands towards heaven, "to speak in sweetest accents the true sentiments of my doating heart, and I cannot fail to gain his faith!"

"Enough," said Henrico, "I have now a request to make of *thee,* lady, on the grant of which depends the issue of thine. Wilt thou suffer me to take the life of Manfred? his death is necessary to my peace of mind."

"Then end him," exclaimed Estifania; "I will conduct thee to the chamber where he lies."

"Rather direct me to it," returned Henrico, "and remain thou here, whilst I go forth to accomplish my design; should we be seen together, thou must be well assured that it would end in ill to both of us."

"Swear that thou lovest me," cried Estifania, catching hold of his hand, "and thy will is mine."

"Did I not love thee," said the youth, "should I thus readily accede to thy proposals?"

"Yes, thou dost love me," cried Estifania, "I see thou dost; may all the raptures of unbounded love be thine! thou soon shalt prove that love reciprocal can be warmed in other breasts besides Matilda's."

"Lose not thus the precious moments," interrupted Henrico; "but quickly describe to me the chamber where Manfred lies."

"Dost thou recollect the passage through which thou wert conveyed hither from the marble hall?" asked Estifania.

"I do."

"Return by them, and cross the western angle of the hall; facing thee thou wilt behold a flight of stairs conducting to a narrow gallery; ascend them, and the first door thou wilt espy on thy right hand, is the apartment of the esquire."

"Thanks!" cried Henrico, "I shall find it."

"Now take this sword," replied the exulting woman; "would I could with it give thee success: my fervent prayers attend thee."

"My friend," said Henrico, "bear thou the lamp."

Alphonso immediately received it from the hand of Estifania, and opened the prison door; Henrico hastily pushed him forwards, followed him, and instantly closing the gate, locked and bolted it.—"Now, my friend, be silent, and follow me," he exclaimed, and they proceeded with cautious steps.

Being arrived in the hall, every indication of a night passed in drunkenness and debauchery presented itself to their view; and some of the revellers, overpowered by wine and sleep, lay scattered on the sofas and carpets which were dispersed about the hall. Henrico, however, perceived that he had nothing to dread from them, as not only their senses appeared to be stupified, but their faculties blunted by the excesses of the night; the friends, therefore, passed on, and ascended the stairs which the beguiled Estifania had pointed out to them; and, according to her instruction, Henrico opened the door of the first apartment on his right hand: he entered, and Alphonso having followed him, closed the door.

Manfred, who in compliance with the promise he had made Estifania of being prepared against any emergency, had only thrown himself on the outside of the bed, immediately sprang up, and was advancing towards the door, when Henrico, seizing him by the throat, and presenting at him his sword, which he had drawn at the instant he left the dungeon, exclaimed—"Silence alone preserves thy life; if thou utter one word, this shall pierce thy heart."

"Vile slave," returned Manfred, somewhat recovered from the surprise into which the unexpected presence of Henrico had thrown him, and was feeling for his sword, when he with the greatest remorse recollected that he had entrusted it to Estifania, and with the fury of a madman, seeing his own weapon lifted against himself, exclaimed—"Cursed harlot! racks and furies rend thy lewd heart!" Then turning to Henrico, he continued—"I am in thy power; use me as thou wilt."

"Thou shewedst no pity unto me," replied the youth, "and therefore deservest none at my hand; yet I will shew thee my heart is not so hardened by the ills which I myself have suffered, as to inflict them wantonly on others. Shew me the apartment where the daughter of the baron of Ollada is confined, and thou hast nought to fear from me."

"Shield me from the fury of the duke," returned the esquire, "and I'll obey thee."

"Hadst thou not," said Henrico, "allured by interest, obeyed his impious commands, but guided by the dictates of that never failing friend, thy conscience, thou hadst spurned the bribe which bound thee to injure unprovoking innocence, thou hadst never stood in awe of such a monster; as it is, thou must abide by the consequence of thy baseness."

So saying, he bound and gagged the struggling Manfred; then dragging him without the chamber, he gave him into the hands of Alphonso, and commanded him to lead the way to Matilda's chamber.

Manfred, finding all resistance he could make in his present situation in vain, proceeded along the gallery, and descending three steps, entered another, much loftier than that they had just left, and elegantly adorned with portraits and embellishments of every kind; he then stopped, and by bowing his head towards a door on the left, signified *that* to be the chamber.

Henrico, who had now both the lamp and sword in his hand, rushed into the apartment, and to his inexpressible astonishment, perceived, on her knees, before the duke of Gonsalez, who was seated on a velvet sofa, Matilda in the most lamentable accents imploring him to have pity on her, whilst the crystal tears flowed fast from her swollen eyes.

The duke, on perceiving Henrico, instantly uttered the most frantic expressions, similar to those which he had made in the hall; and foregoing the hand of Matilda, which had been pressed to his devouring lips, hid his face in his mantle.

Henrico, waving his hand to his friend and Matilda to be silent, locked the door of the apartment, and beckoning to Alphonso to assist him in stripping off the outward garments of the duke, they then bound him with the linen which composed Henrico's sash, and cutting off a portion of the tough sheath of his sword, they gagged him therewith: they now unbound Manfred, and having taken off his cloak and upper garments, they rebound his arms, and laid him extended on the floor. Henrico then clad himself in the habiliments of the duke, and Alphonso dressed himself in those of the esquire, and throwing off their own furred caps, they put on the feathered hats of their vanquished enemies.

Henrico now threw open the sash, and perceiving that they were raised not above five feet at most from the ground, informed his companions that he judged it most expedient for them to enter the court-yard which surrounded the castle, by vaulting from this window, rather than to hazard a discovery from the revellers in the hall, some of whom might perchance be awakened; accordingly he vaulted from the window, and Matilda, forgetting all danger in the midst of her alarm, dauntlessly sprang into his extended arms. Alphonso now threw out Henrico's sword, and having girt that of the duke on his own side, hastily followed the panting lovers.

Matilda, according to Henrico's instruction, appeared to proceed with reluctance, whilst Alphonso and himself seemed to drag her along. When they approached near the outward wall of the court-yard, the guards, deceived by the garments which the two friends wore, instantly drew up the portcullis, and threw open the heavy gates; having passed through, amidst the most humble salutations of the vassals, they heard the gates again shut; being arrived near the drawbridge, they found that it was guarded by two men only, who were sleeping beneath the shade of the uplifted bridge. Alphonso having hailed them, they, starting suddenly from sleep, and recognising the habits of the duke and his esquire, instantly let fall the bridge, and the friends passed over quickly in silence.

A few faintly shining stars afforded them a slender gleam of light, and they walked on for the space of half a league, without speaking; when Matilda, recollecting that Villetta was left behind, began to express her concern for her faithful servant, to her companions. Henrico used all the arguments in his power to prove that Villetta had nothing to fear at the castle, as the duke would not condescend to revenge himself on a helpless girl, if even he knew of her being in his power, which was very doubtful, and entreated Matilda to make herself easy on that account; his words had so great weight with her, that her apprehensions for Villetta soon began to be greatly diminished.

When they had proceeded rather more than half a league farther, over a heathy ground, on which brambles and low bushes grew thick and irregular, and through which there was no direct path, Henrico, on whose arm Matilda was leaning, stopped, and thrusting his hand into what appeared to be the withered trunk of a tree, drew from thence a small tucket, which he sounded; the sound was instantly answered by another, seemingly under ground: Henrico, upon hearing this, blew a shrill whistle. No sooner had he done so, than the earth seemed to open, and presented to their view a flight of steps, conducting to a cave, which appeared to be illumined by a light at some distance within it. Henrico immediately let down Matilda; and Alphonso having followed them, the entrance was again closed.

The youth now conducted Matilda through a long passage, cut out of the earth, and lighted by a lamp which hung from its top. At this, Henrico lighted a lamp, which he had taken from a niche in the side of the passage, and having proceeded a few steps farther, opened a door, which presented to their sight a wooden staircase; this they ascended, and arrived in an apartment which wore the appearance of the greatest desolation, and which was entirely without furniture; from this they entered another, in which was a bed that seemed once to have been formed of costly materials; near it stood a small table of hazel wood, a chair covered with purple velvet, and another of garnet-coloured satin. "Now, lady," exclaimed the young peasant, "let me congratulate you on having escaped all danger, and let me bless the kind fates that have made me the instrument of your preservation."

"I cannot attempt to thank thee," replied Matilda; "words would fail me to express my gratitude. But, I conjure thee, tell me where I am?"

"Where you have nought to fear, dearest lady, and in the midst of those that would protect you at the peril of their lives. Let this reply content you, dearest love, till sleep shall have repaired your wasting strength; let no vain fears, I entreat you, interrupt your slumbers. Fasten yourself within this chamber; I will watch meanwhile in the outer apartment."

"I am but ill disposed to sleep," rejoined Matilda; "my spirits must be more composed, and somewhat weaned from the recollection of my late terrors, ere I can hope to taste repose. Therefore, if thou lovest me, I pray thee inform me where I now am, and unto whom I owe my safety?"

Henrico, finding that she wished not to retire to the bed which had been prepared for her reception, persuaded her to descend into a small apartment, formed out of a part of the cavern, where a sprightly wood fire was burning on the hearth; and having drawn her a stool near the clay chimney, he seated himself by her: and after he had informed her of the fortunate manner in which he and his friend had that night escaped from their prison in the duke of Gonsalez's castle, related to her his story in the following words.

CHAPTER VI

She loved me for the dangers I had past,
And I lov'd her that she did pity them.
Othello.

"THE man, dearest Matilda, who now addresses you, derives the only merit of his life from having been in some degree serviceable to so unfortunate a lady. From family, he derives no glory, being to this moment ignorant of his progenitors; from his actions, no honour, they having been always concealed; would they could be hidden even from my own heart! the recollection of them stings me to the soul, though I never, save when constrained by force, engaged in them. Pardon me, lady, that I preface the short detail of my solitary life by these complaints, I had forgot myself; now, hear my melancholy tale.

The first I can remember is, that I found myself in this cave amongst a troop of men, whose countenances were clouded with the sullen gloom of dissatisfaction; on the brow of some amongst them, the frown of brutality and cruelty were strongly depicted. In that division of the cave where I dragged on a solitary existence, to me by no means irksome, for I knew no other, the greatest part of my companions spent their time over their cups and dice; they gamed, as I afterwards found, for large sums. This but too often raised quarrels amongst them, which were always productive of inveterate animosities, and sometimes of bloodshed.

During the first five years of which I have any remembrance, I remarked that a certain number of these men regularly retired at a particular hour of the day, to a part of the cave which I had never seen, and remained there several hours. Happening one day to be alone with one of the men, named Isidor, to whom I had always felt myself more strongly attached than to any of the others, I could not forbear inquiring of him who I was? who were the persons that I constantly saw around me, and what was their occupation? I had already learnt from the conversation of my companions, that money, the great passport, not less to every luxury than to every necessary of life, was to be obtained only by labour, and that the world abounded with men of various professions, for the purpose of obtaining it. He answered me with a smile, that they were a set of noble free-hearted men, who, being wearied by the enforcement of laws and the restraint of customs, to which he informed me the inhabitants of the great world were subject, had resolved on passing away their lives in an undisturbed and happy obscurity: "this cavern," continued he, "is unknown to any one but those who inhabit it; and you may thank Heaven for having conferred on you the greatest happiness it can bestow on a mortal, in having placed you here." The manner in which he uttered this sentence, and the reserve which I read in his countenance, raised my curiosity to the highest pitch; and wishing, if possible, to gain some farther information, I asked him, humouring his own conceit, by what happy chance I came hither?

"It is now near nine years," replied Isidor, "since, as my comrade Alphonso and myself were walking in a small wood, not far distant from this cavern, we imagined we heard a child cry; we listened, and the sounds continuing, we approached towards the spot whence they proceeded: we perceived a flannel mantle, wrapped up closely, lying on the ground; we took it up, opened it, and therein found you, at that time, as nearly as we could guess, an infant of about fifteen months old. Alphonso took you in his arms, and after we had expressed our mutual surprise at this extraordinary adventure, we consulted how we should act concerning you: at length we resolved to carry you to our habitation; and, as we had no woman amongst us, to nurse you ourselves, with all the care we were able, leaving to Providence whether to take or spare your life, which appeared to be nearly exhausted by hunger and crying. When we arrived at the cave, we found our companions at their midday repast; they rallied us, and would not be persuaded but that you were the child either of Alphonso or myself, the fruit of our intercourse with some girl in the neighbourhood; nor did they forget to upbraid us for exposing ourselves to a discovery, for the sake of gratifying our boyish desires. We then informed them of the manner in which we found you, and having solemnly declared we had not taken any steps which might be likely to discover our dwelling, and lastly, having sworn firm allegiance to our comrades, they became persuaded of our innocence, and expressed equal astonishment with ourselves at so unwonted an occurrence; they advised us to unwrap you, and examine whether there was not, perchance, any trinket or paper concealed in the folds of the mantle, which might inform us who you were. After we had somewhat satisfied your craving appetite, we carefully searched the robe, but found nothing which could in the least gratify our curiosity. Alphonso then took upon himself the office of nurse, and lulled you to sleep; he, in particular, attended to you with never-failing care and anxiety; Heaven forwarded his endeavours, and you, in a short time, became strong and healthy, having perfectly recovered what you had suffered during your exposure in the wood."

This was all I ever heard from Isidor; one of the troop entering at that moment, he was prevented from proceeding, and I had not an opportunity of again questioning him before his death, which, to my inexpressible concern, happened very suddenly, not many days after our conversation.

The kind Alphonso now began to instruct me in many branches of science and useful knowledge; from the few books he possessed, he taught me reading, and also found means to instruct me in the art of writing; where he was deficient in books, his rhetoric made ample amends. My days were now spent in attending to his instructions; he stored my mind with a fund of precepts of inestimable value, preparatory, as I then thought, to my making my first entrance on the busy stage of life. Delusive hope! how little did I imagine I was doomed to live in an eternal seclusion from the world!

I was frequently favoured by walking with my indulgent friend; I call him so, for he has truly proved himself such, in that wood where he snatched me from the jaws of death. Unhappy deliverance! but that Heaven had destined me to rescue thee, lady, and be rewarded for all the dangers I have undergone, by thy approving smiles.

About this time, the captain of the band dying, Alphonso succeeded him in authority, and was now always one of those who retired to the secret part of the cave. Not long after this, Alphonso finding me one day alone, in a separate division of the cavern, thus addressed me—"You must, I think, Henrico, since you have arrived at years of discernment, have marvelled within yourself, although you have prudently forborn to mention your surprise, that men, who seem formed for fulfilling useful stations in life, in which they might acquit themselves to their credit and advantage, and for enjoying that society which is to be met with in the world at large, should have secluded themselves from it, on the plea of leading tranquil and retired lives, free from those cares to which they would have been more or less exposed in it. This, I understand, is the reason which has been already given you for our inhabiting this dreary abode; this cause we had all agreed to assign, in case you interrogated any one of us, as we knew not, but, that ignorant of the advantages of your situation, you might, perchance, by some means, effect your escape from this place, and betray us. The time is now come that you are to be made acquainted with the true cause of our seclusion; but you must first swear inviolable secrecy and strict allegiance to our band."

At these words I felt a greater degree of curiosity and surprise dart through my heart than my suspicions had ever yet produced, and I answered him that I would readily and gratefully comply with his demand. Upon this he produced a paper, on which were written the names of all the troop, and desired me to add mine: I obeyed him, and having taken the oath which he had required of me, he told me to follow him; I did so. He proceeded to that spot in the cavern which had so frequently excited my curiosity, and taking a key from his pocket, he opened the door and we entered.

The first object on which I cast my eyes, was a large furnace; round the cavern were fixed tables, upon which lay dispersed pieces of bullion, hammers, screws, saws, and several other tools; in one corner stood two iron chests; Alphonso approached towards them, and, taking another key from his pocket, unlocked the larger of the two, and threw open the lid; guess my astonishment at beholding it nearly filled with pistoles—"There, youth," exclaimed Alphonso, "now say, whether we, who can supply ourselves with any quantity of these, are not happy, in comparison to the inhabitants of the great world, who, after days of toil, and nights of waking, can barely supply the wants of nature, when *we* have never-failing sources for procuring every luxury life can afford us?—I see thou art about to ask me, how we came by this?—we forge it, boy! I will instruct thee how to make it at thy will."—"Wilt thou then also teach me," returned I, trembling at the thought of the oath which had bound me to the commission of a deed, from which I instantly recoiled, "to steel my heart against the stings of conscience, unto which this sin will subject me?" Alphonso seemed sensibly to feel the reproach I had glanced at him, but smiling, he cried—"Talk not thus, Henrico; thou art much deceived in thinking this a crime; we rob no one by it, nay, far from that, the circulation of the coin we make, cannot fail to benefit mankind."—"Then," said I, "why, my friend, do you thus act in secret? if what you do is of advantage to men, why do you not openly avow it, and receive the applauses due to your industry?"—"'Tis necessary, youth," replied Alphonso, "that our coin should not be known from that which passes current in the kingdom, by the sanction of the king."—"Is it not then," said I, "meant to resemble that?"—"With the greatest exactness," he answered.—"Thou hast already taught me," I returned, "that the hearts of men are swayed by two ruling principles, virtue and vice—that in the former are centered all noble and praiseworthy qualities—in the latter, the contrary to these—and in this class I cannot hesitate to rank deceit."—"Hark!" exclaimed Alphonso, "I hear our comrades approaching to their daily task; this day they have appointed to instruct thee in the art which we possess; for thine own sake and mine, I conjure thee to seem reconciled to thy situation. I will converse with thee anon in private."

The band now entered, and having congratulated me on my initiation into the mysteries of the cavern, heated the furnace and began their operations, in which I was obliged, Heaven knows with how great reluctance, to assist with the most apparent readiness. After three hundred pieces had been formed and stamped, they left that part of the cavern; and Alphonso, having locked the door, and returned the key into his pocket, beckoned me to follow him into the wood. I immediately complied with his signal.

When we were alone, Alphonso thus addressed me—"Think not, Henrico, that I am about to chide thee for the sentiments thou hast expressed, far be such a thought from me; after the instructions, which, to the best of my ability, I have given thee, it would not less have grieved than surprised me, to have found thy nature other than it is. As captain of this band, I was bound by oath to make the discovery of the secrets of this cavern unto thee in the manner I did; but be assured, now that task is fulfilled, I never again will urge thee on the subject. Believe me, youth, it joys my heart to find thy sentiments congenial with my own." I now asked him, since he held the practices of our companions in equal abhorrence with myself, what could have induced him to league with them?—"Alas!" replied Alphonso, "compulsion drove me to it; it is a penance far inferior to a crime of blackest die, that lies full heavy on my heart. A noble mind like thine, would, I well know, disdain to betray a wretch like me, and on that assurance I would confide to thee the source of all my sufferings, had I not called on Heaven to pour its vengeance on me, if e'er, except on one condition only, I revealed my guilt." Perceiving a tear, which he strove to suppress, starting in his eye, I forbore to question him further, and in a short time we returned to the cavern.

The band now informed me that the greatest part of our solitary dwelling, ran under a building which was called the Castle of Ollada, and that it had for some time been uninhabited, owing to a report sedulously published by them of its being haunted; that they had two private passages, by which four of the troop ascended every night into one of its galleries, in order to seize on any traveller who might be driven to take shelter in it from a storm, or any other person, who, from curiosity, might be induced to visit it, and force them down into the cavern, thus to intimidate others from approaching the castle, and consequently from discovering their haunt; they added, that they had never yet taken any one except a priest, who died ere he had been a month among them.

I was now obliged to take my turn in watching, but fortunately, as I thought, we did not find that any one visited the castle, at least those parts in which my companions had any thing to apprehend from them, as there were no communications with this cavern in any other part of the castle. The name of the castle, the reason of its being uninhabited, and the family to whom it belonged, Alphonso had long before acquainted me with.

From this time I recollect nothing worth recording, until that fortunate evening, when, having strayed somewhat beyond our usual bounds, striving to sooth not less my own melancholy than that of my friend, by the melody of a shepherd's pipe, which he had taught me to sound, I first beheld thee, my dearest Matilda. I had rarely before that happy day seen a female; if by chance a rustic girl had met my sight, I had beheld her with the eye of cold indifference; but, oh! what were my feelings, while in silent rapture I gazed on thee!—the eloquence of an angel would seem but faintly to describe them. When you cast your eyes towards me, methought they opened to me the inmost recesses of your heart, and that I therein read engraved, *perfection.* With what unwillingness did I slowly tread back the steps that led me from you! at my return, a doubly dismal gloom seemed to obscure our dreary cavern. After a long and sleepless night, I rose to a more irksome morn; whichever way I turned, my eyes beheld a vacancy, which e'en your loved idea could but slenderly fill up, the substance still was wanting—Matilda's self was absent.

With the greatest eagerness I every day returned to the spot; but, alas! I saw you no more, until that evening when Alphonso and myself delivered you from the duke's cowardly vassals; how did I bless the hour that enabled me to render you that seasonable service. Six weeks now passed away, and as I had constantly visited the wood without seeing you, I almost despaired of beholding you again.

About this time a circumstance occurred, which I must relate to you. Four of our band, whose turn it was to watch in the castle, resolved, as they afterwards informed us, on spending the hours of their watch over their dice; and that they might not be surprised whilst thus engaged, they locked the two doors leading into the gallery from the apartments in which they were, and taking their station in the room nearest the gallery, that they might hear any noise in that part of the castle, one of them hung up his mantle before the casement, to prevent the light of their lamp being so plainly seen by any one who might happen to be passing along the road bordering on the forest; two nights they had held their watch in this apartment, without taking this precaution; on the third, they were startled about midnight, by a loud rapping at the door of the apartment, which was immediately followed by a voice, but their alarm prevented them from distinguishing the words it uttered; the three who heard it having awakened their companion, who was snoring in the corner of the room, they all proceeded through a narrow passage, which ran between the suite of chambers and the gallery, and having opened the other door at the end of it, entered the gallery, and perceiving two men, one of whom was a friar, standing at a small distance from them, rushed upon them, and instantly dragged them down into the cavern. The two unhappy men, overcome by terror and surprise at finding themselves seized, from a quarter they so little expected, made not the least resistance nor uttered a single cry.

One of the band having now roused all his companions, Alphonso began to question the innocent prisoners, when the friar, entreating for mercy, informed us, that in consequence of a light having two nights before appeared through a casement of the castle, he and his friend, whom he called Perez, had from curiosity visited it; he told us that his name was Anselm, that he was a brother of the neighbouring monastery of Maqueda, and that his companion was the steward of Garcia, baron of Ollada; they both, in the most lamentable strains, implored us to release them, swearing not to betray the band, on condition of our granting them their liberty. My friend Alphonso seemed inclinable to trust them; but our comrades testifying their strong disapprobation of his intention, they have never since that night stirred a single step from the cavern. Father Anselm appears to have become tolerably well reconciled to his situation; Perez expresses great dissatisfaction, and is seemingly in continual alarm.

When night arrived, four other men ascended into the castle, and on their return in the morning, informed Alphonso that they had seen no one that night, but had found the lock cut out of the door of the apartment in which their companions had watched the preceding night. Alphonso immediately ordered the lock to be replaced, and interrogated father Anselm, whether he had brought with him to the castle any other person beside Perez. The holy man confessed that a youth had accompanied them, who had rapped at the door of the apartment, whilst himself and the old steward had remained at a short distance.

Our captain, on hearing this, as he conjectured that the prisoner's friend might, on that or some succeeding night, return to the castle, with a great number of the baron of Ollada's vassals, whom they could have no chance of securing, informed us, that he thought the most advisable method of proceeding was, if possible, to terrify any persons who might in future visit the castle, and expressed his wish that one of us would for that purpose take the watch alone, habited in a manner to give the idea of a dreadful spectre.

As this plan appeared to me far preferable to the measures which had before been adopted, and perceiving that no one was very ready to comply with Alphonso's request, I offered my services, which were gratefully accepted. Accordingly when night came, clad in bloody rags, my legs and arms bound with heavy chains, which apparently fastened them to my body, with a burning lamp fixed on my head, and a sword girt beneath my garments, in case I should stand in need of it to defend myself, having passed through one of the private passages, I entered the castle.

The first night of my disguise passed away without any interruption; on the next, after I had been about two hours at my post, I imagined I heard voices in the hall of the castle; I approached to the top of the stone staircase and listened; I soon found that the persons whom I heard were the duke of Gonsalez, and his esquire Manfred, who had been driven thither for shelter, in their return from the castle of the duke of Apella, and that his vassals were waiting without with his horses: they had no light with them, and I confess, on recollecting my own situation, I trembled lest they should discover me by the lamp which was burning on my head, and I was going to retire softly from the spot, where I had been attending to their conversation, when I perceived the duke run towards and catch hold of a person with a lanthorn in his hand, who at that moment entered the hall by a gate opposite to the one near which the duke and Manfred had been standing.

The exact words of the discourse which passed between the duke and the baron of Ollada, for he it was who entered the hall, I do not recollect; the substance thereof I will relate unto thee. The duke, on perceiving the person to be thy father, expressed his astonishment at meeting him in this uninhabited castle, in the depth of the night, at the same time informing him of the reason of *his* being there: the baron, seemingly stung to the heart at being thus discovered, instantly besought him, as he hoped to regain his friendship, not to inform any one of his having seen him in this castle; the duke promised he would not, provided he made him acquainted with the cause which had brought him thither. Thy father, Garcia, then entreated Gaspero not to urge him in vain to discover a secret, which he would never disclose, save with his dying breath; and declared that he would reward the secrecy he required of him, by the grant of any other request he should make; he at the same time presented a purse to the esquire, which Manfred perfectly understanding its meaning, bowed significantly and received. The duke then demanded of the baron thy hand in marriage, declaring that to be the only condition on which he would comply with his entreaty. Garcia, after a momentary silence, answered, "She is thine: let me now, I beseech you, retire until you have left the castle."—"I am content," replied the duke; "do as thou wilt; I will not betray thee." Thy father now left the hall, by the same gate at which he had entered.

The duke immediately told Manfred, that he believed the storm was much abated, and ordered him to step out and hail the vassals, who were taking shelter with the horses beneath the trees. The moment I saw the duke alone, I flew down the stairs, and exclaimed—"Forbear, rash Gaspero, to persist in making the daughter of the baron of Ollada thy wife, or prepare thyself to meet my vengeance." Having said these words, I instantly reascended into the gallery, and looking down, found that the duke had left the hall; knowing that I could quickly elude his search, in case he returned with his vassals in pursuit of me, of which I was notwithstanding somewhat apprehensive, I ventured to remain where I then was. In a few minutes the baron again entered the hall by the eastern gate, and having drawn up a panel in the side of the wall, he went in, and closed it after him. I resolved to await the event of a circumstance which had excited in me no small degree of curiosity; within the space of half-an-hour, I saw thy father cautiously open the panel and come out; he then replaced it, and left the castle.

The next morning I seized the first opportunity which offered itself of taking Alphonso apart, and informing him of the scene I had witnessed, which excited his surprise no less than it had mine. I then asked permission of Alphonso to offer you an asylum in this cavern, to which, at length, after many entreaties on my part, he consented; and I, in the warmest terms, expressed my gratitude to him for this kindness.

A difficulty, which had not before entered my thoughts, now started up; this was, how I should be able to obtain a conference with you. I knew no method which offered the slightest probability of success, unless I could by chance see you that evening in the wood; with that hope I watched there an hour, before and after your usual time of walking, but, alas! I saw you not. Disappointed beyond description, I began to despair of rescuing you from the vile duke, when the following expedient suddenly arose in my harassed mind—to throw off my disguise as soon as I entered the castle for the purpose of watching, and fly to the mansion of your father, resolving to station myself within view of it, in expectation of seeing some one of the baron's servants, whom I might bribe to deliver you a letter, which I determined previously to write. I accordingly did so, and having waited near the mansion for above two hours without seeing any one, I ventured to approach the wall of the adjoining garden. I had not been there many minutes ere I heard some one sigh deeply; I listened, and heard a voice, which I could not hesitate to pronounce yours, exclaim, "Unhappy Matilda!" Love lent me strength, and in a moment I scaled the wall; of what followed I need not inform you.

Alphonso, when I the next morning acquainted him with my unexpected good fortune, chid me for the rashness of which he said I had been guilty, but quickly forgave me, in consideration of my conduct having been productive of no ill consequences. How widely different a plea for his forgiveness would he have found, had his feelings been consonant with mine! In compliance with my request, he informed the band of our wish to afford you our protection; upon which they all voluntarily bound themselves by oath to protect and defend you.

To describe my agony of mind on revisiting the spot where you had appointed to meet me the next night, I will not attempt; the only picture which presented itself to my distracted imagination, was my beloved Matilda struggling in the hated arms of the remorseless duke, and calling on Heaven to assist her. So strongly did this idea operate on my mind, that although, upon the return of my reason, I shrunk within myself at the recollection of my crimes, I cursed the unfeeling hand of Heaven, that had not worked a miracle in thy behalf!"

Matilda could not here forbear interrupting Henrico, to acquaint him with the perverse accident which had prevented her from fulfilling her promise; she also expressed her surprise at what he had related concerning her father, and inquired whether he had ever seen the baron come to the castle, beside the night which he had mentioned? He told her that he had never held the watch after that night, and begged leave of her to proceed in his narration; she answered him that it was her earnest desire he would do so; upon which he thus continued:—

"The good Alphonso, perceiving with pity the distress of my mind, on the next day promised to make an attempt himself at gaining some information relative to you; accordingly, having dressed himself in a friar's habit, which he borrowed from father Anselm, he about noon left the cavern: on his return, some two hours after, he told me that he had met with an old wood-cutter in the forest, whom he knew to be one of the baron's tenants, and having entered into conversation with him, inquired, amongst other questions, whether the baron of Ollada's daughter was not that day wedded to the duke of Gonsalez, and that the old man answered in the negative, saying, that he had heard the baron held a great feast on the evening of that day, in honour of his daughter's intended nuptials.

The next morning, my worthy friend again went out in the same habit, and seeing a great concourse of people flocking towards the baron's residence, inquired what drew them thither, and being answered that a tournament was that day held on the green before thy father's mansion, he resolved, under favour of his habit, to be a spectator himself; and returning about midday, informed me that the duke was singly sweeping away all the honours of the field.

Stung by this account, I conjured him to assume another disguise for my sake, and carry a challenge to the haughty Gaspero from me, as from a knight desirous of concealing his name. Alphonso used all the arguments he could frame to discourage me from an undertaking accompanied with so great danger; but perceiving that nothing he said could in the least shake my resolution, he habited himself in an esquire's dress, and set out with the billet I had written, which having delivered, he immediately returned.

With what eagerness did I look forward to the day on which I hoped to vanquish my detested rival! With what rapture did my heart bound, when I mounted the steed Alphonso had procured for me! There were no horses belonging to the band, as our companions always rode on mules in their journies to Toledo, for procuring such commodities as the troop stood in need of. Alphonso, as thou wilt easily suppose, was the esquire who attended me.

If I felt joy in the *hope* of overcoming the duke, what were my transports when I saw him fall at my feet! Yet I could not suppose him so severely wounded as he appeared to be, knowing that the thick helmet which he wore must greatly have lightened the blow of my spear; Alphonso was of the same opinion; and no sooner were we arrived in safety at our abode, than that generous man, indefatigable in his attempts at serving one for whom he professed a friendship, declared his intention of immediately setting out for Gaspero's castle, which thou knowest is about a league distant from this cave, and feigning himself a palmer, to ask alms of the duke, hoping, by these means, to gain some information from the domestics.

Alphonso's plan succeeded so far, that he learnt from the discourse of the vassals, that their lord was not so severely wounded as they had imagined, although he had been at first much stunned. He also heard several circumstances, which, however trivial in themselves, led me to suspect that the duke had some private reason for his deceitful conduct—perhaps to try the strength of his mistress's affection, when she considered the dangers to which he had exposed himself for her sake. I accordingly mounted the swiftest mule our stable could afford, resolving, if possible, to see you that night, and if I failed therein, again to make an attempt at getting a letter delivered into your hands. It was midnight ere I approached your father's mansion, and when I came within sight of it, I plainly perceived the baron come out, and strike into the path leading to the castle of Ollada. His absence gave me fresh courage, and having rode up to the mansion, and seeing a light shine through one of the windows, I ventured to pronounce your name. The reason of my requesting you to draw up my letter was, that I feared to risk a conversation in a place where we were so liable to a discovery.

With all the circumstances subsequent to that time you are acquainted, except the manner by which I learnt that Garcia had decreed this night to deliver you up to the duke. This I overheard the esquire Manfred tell his companions, as they this evening passed Alphonso and myself in the forest, as we were coming to conduct you to our solitary abode."

CHAPTER VII

————————Even-handed Justice
Returns th' ingredients of our poison'd chalice
To our own lips.

Macbeth.

MATILDA, no longer ignorant of the reason which had produced the phrenzy of the duke, on his seeing Henrico, extended her hands to heaven, and blessed the all-wise Power that had so miraculously delivered her from the licentious Gaspero; she again thanked her preserver for the anxious concern he had taken in her welfare, and far from bewailing the gloom of that abode, of which she now considered herself an inhabitant for life, and at the idea of which she would in any other circumstances have shuddered, she viewed it with as great delight as she would have beheld a paradise, when compared to the castle of the duke of Gonsalez.

Henrico having now prevailed on her to retire to rest, of which she stood greatly in need, after the fatigues to which she had that night been exposed, lighted her to the upper apartment, which he had fitted up for her with such furniture as he had collected from the deserted castle, and having entreated her to compose herself to sleep, and renewed his promise of remaining meanwhile in the outer apartment, he gave her the lamp, and she closed the door; sleep soon overcame her wearied frame, and having thrown herself on the outside of the bed, she sunk into a refreshing slumber.

Day was just beginning to dawn, when Alphonso entered the apartment, where Henrico was guarding his dear Matilda, and thus addressed him.—"Henrico, a circumstance of a very disagreeable nature, and which I much fear to be the omen of our retreat being discovered, has last night occurred; the agitation of your mind, yesterday, prevented me from informing you, that the night before last, our comrade, who held the watch in the castle, found a youth in one of the apartments, who seemed but little alarmed at the appearance of our friend in his disguise, and still more unwilling to leave the room, which our companion pointed to him to do; that when the youth had done so, he secured the outward door leading from the gallery through the suite of apartments to our secret passage, and having uttered some words calculated, if possible, to inspire him with fear, immediately descended into the cave. Judging it to be the youth who had some time before accompanied the holy father and the baron's steward thither, what had happened gave me but little concern, as I found that he had returned alone: another of the band had the watch last night, when eager to hear if any thing had occurred, I inquired for him about half an hour ago, and being told that he was not yet come back to the cavern, I sent two others of our comrades in search of him, who in a short time returned and informed me, that they had found him lying just without the trap-door, which opens into our private passage, lifeless, and weltering in his blood."

The friends had now been together for nearly two hours, expressing their mutual astonishment at the recent occurrence, and forming conjectures, to none of which they could assign any great degree of probability, when they heard a tumult of voices and a clashing of swords, in the lower part of the cavern; they instantly rose and ran towards that part from whence the noise proceeded: arrived there, they beheld their companions, nine in number, bravely opposing some armed men, who were descending into the cavern from the trap-door in the castle; they at the same moment perceived father Anselm and Perez run towards a youth who seemed to head the assailing troop, and exclaim—"Oh! my good master, brave, noble lord Altador, do I then behold you once again, my dearest master?" Henrico, immediately upon this, knew these men to be the vassals of the baron of Ollada, and the youth who commanded them to be his nephew, and seeing three of the band lying dead, and four already bound, gave himself up for lost.

Alphonso perceiving his emotion, thus addressed him, in a low voice—"Name not Matilda, I conjure you, but confide in me." Having said this, he immediately gave himself up to be bound, as did Henrico, following his friend's example; they then all left the cavern, by the entrance upon the forest, which Alphonso voluntarily pointed out to Altador.

Henrico's reflections on the distress of Matilda when she should awake and find him gone, and his ignorance of his friend's reason for his extraordinary conduct, into which he had no opportunity of inquiring, produced an agony of mind, under which all his fortitude could scarcely support him.

It is now necessary to inform the reader, that on the day following the duke's overthrow at the tournament, it had been concerted between him and the baron, that if the baron received a message that evening from the duke, importing that he was much mended, and wished to see the baron on the following day, which message the reader will recollect to have been delivered to Garcia during supper, Gaspero would that night send his esquire Manfred to conduct Matilda to his castle, would marry her on the following morning and expect her father to visit her as duchess of Gonsalez.

The baron, at the usual hour, retired to his chamber, having commanded Lopez, on the arrival of Manfred, to call up Matilda, telling her that her father wished to see her immediately in the hall, and on her descending, to deliver her to the duke's vassals.

Lopez, finding she had left the mansion, besought Manfred to pursue her immediately, and carefully concealed the circumstance from the baron, lest his diligence should have been called in question, and informed him that his daughter had been carried away by the duke's vassals, according to the preconcerted plan.

The baron, accordingly, at an early hour, attended by six of his vassals and his esquire Octavio, set out for the duke's castle. Surprised at finding the drawbridge down, the gates open, and the whole castle apparently in confusion, he entered, and inquired for Manfred; one of the domestics answered, that Manfred had that morning fallen by the duke's own hand.—"Where is the duke?" asked Garcia.

The vassal proceeded to an apartment, the door of which was open; the baron and Octavio entered. The first object that met their astonished sight was the duke, raving like a madman over the dying body of Estifania, whom he had just stabbed, and heaping curses on her for having drawn down ruin on herself and him by her ungoverned lust.—"What means this phrensy?" cried Garcia; "where is my child?"

"Seek her amongst her cullies, ask her of those with whom she holds her midnight revels," returned the duke.

"Stain not my chaste, my virtuous child with these aspersions," exclaimed the baron, "but instantly explain thyself."

"Hoary dissembler," answered Gaspero, the foam gushing from his lips, "there's not a hind in all Ollada, but has been glutted with her charms—thou knowest it well; but thou art false as she is, and she as hell; get thee thither and seek her, thou damned traitor." So saying, he snatched a dagger from his side, and plunged it into the shoulder of Garcia; fortunately, the baron's

117

wound was not in his right arm; in an instant he drew his sword, pierced the duke's heart, and immediately fainted through loss of blood.

The duke survived but a few moments, and breathed his last in heavy curses and dreadful imprecations on the baron and Matilda.

The fainting baron was, with all convenient speed, brought back to his own mansion. Father Francisco and father Benedict were immediately sent for to receive his confession, and pray with him. Father Carlos, one of the brothers of the monastery, skilled in physic, also attended, who pronounced the wound to be mortal.

Altador, who had not been long arrived with his prisoners, was instantly admitted to the baron; and having informed him of what had happened, and that one of the coiners, named Alphonso, had declared he had something of the greatest importance to communicate to him, Alphonso was accordingly sent for into his chamber, and left alone with him an hour, at the expiration of which time he set out with two of the baron's vassals to the cavern in search of Matilda.

She, overcome with fatigue, had found sleep too welcome a visitant to be speedily shaken off, and was still on the bed. On being informed of what had happened in the cave, she, on her knees, implored Alphonso not to deliver her up to her father's resentment: but her fears instantly subsided when she heard that the duke was no more; and on the account Alphonso gave her of her father's situation, she forgot his cruelties, and thought only of serving him.

Matilda arrived at her father's mansion, and was received with open arms by the affectionate Hypolita, who conducted her immediately to the baron's chamber, whither they were followed by Altador, Henrico, and Alphonso. Garcia, in a transport of joy, folded his daughter in his arms, exclaiming—"Oh! my Matilda, canst thou forgive an unfeeling father, driven by desperation to inflict cruelties on his child? Heaven, I trust, has preserved thee to enjoy that uninterrupted happiness which I have never tasted."

Matilda's tears prevented her utterance.

"And thou, youth," continued the baron, addressing himself to Henrico, "come near; and if the blessing of a wretch like me can profit thee, Heaven in its mercy reward thee according to thy merit, in having preserved a sister from the miseries to which an unhappy father had doomed her."

"Sister!" stammered out Henrico, and gazed first at Alphonso then at the baron.

Garcia thus proceeded—"I have heard thy story from Alphonso—Oh! curse not thy father on his deathbed, but I was that inhuman monster that begot and then exposed thee."

Henrico fell on his knees, and seizing the baron's hand, fervently kissed it. The baron then embraced him, and they both shed tears.

"My brother! my deliverer!" cried Matilda, throwing her arms in an ecstacy round Henrico's neck. "Oh! my father, explain this mystery."

"Alphonso will do that when I am gone," returned the baron; "for pity harass not my last moments by a recital of acts, which I would freely give the riches of the world to have undone."

Matilda reclined her head on Hypolita's bosom; the baron thus went on—"Altador, while yet I have the power, take the confession of my deceit to thee; know then, that what I uttered unto thee in my last illness, proceeded from my heart. Alphonso now will perform the task I then asked of thee; but do thou accompany him to the castle, and you, my children, and you, kind lady; take Lopez also with you—he knows my most private concerns. Altador, thou art the rightful heir of the castle—inherit it, and be blessed; I basely robbed thee of it—that is the least injury I have done thee, as thou wilt find hereafter; but curse me not when I am dead—say thou forgivest me, that I may strive, the few moments I have to live, to make my peace on high."

"May Heaven forgive thee as I do," cried Altador, and then embraced him.

Father Francisco now came forward—"Pardon me," he said, "but I must request a moment's audience, in the presence of these friends. Dost thou not, Garcia, recollect that Rosala, ere she became the wife of Hugo, bore a child unto thee?"

"I do; knowest thou ought of him—is he not dead?" eagerly asked the baron.

"Behold him now before thee," returned Francisco, taking Altador by the hand.

"Overwhelm me not with these discoveries," exclaimed the baron, and sunk upon his pillow: Altador flew towards the bed, and caught his father in his arms.—"How canst thou assure me of this?" cried the baron, again opening his eyes.

"You must remember," returned the holy man, "that thy child was said to have died, whilst the infant of thy brother Ferdinand was at nurse with Rosala; but on her deathbed she confessed to me, that she had taken the horrid resolution of murdering thy brother's child, and returning her own in its stead; that accordingly she took the child into a wood, for the purpose of more privately executing her design, but being touched with remorse when there, she resolved to leave it exposed, hoping some passenger might take compassion on it; and returning to the spot the next day, she found it gone, and had never heard of it since.

"Blessed be Heaven," cried the baron, "then I have not injured thee, my child, since thou *art* mine; Henrico and thou shalt share my fortunes; but, oh! look with an anxious eye on my Matilda, and my friend Hypolita."

Father Carlos now entreated them to leave the chamber, as he perceived the baron's last moments were fast approaching— they accordingly descended into the lower apartment.

"Oh! Altador," cried Matilda, "wilt thou now blame me for having concealed from thee the fatal secret, with which father Francisco had so wisely intrusted me?"

He embraced her in silence—his heart was too full to give utterance to his feelings.

Alphonso was engaged in acquainting the lady Hypolita with the transactions of the preceding night, which, when he had concluded, he requested Altador to inform him in what manner he had discovered their retreat.

Altador then told him, that after he had fallen through the sliding door, he overheard, from the conversation of some of the band, who were sitting in a division of the cavern, near the spot where he fell, what the spectre was which he had seen, and what was the occupation of the inhabitants of the cavern; and having found that another of the troop was to ascend the next night, he hid himself, during the whole of the succeeding day, in a dark corner of the cave, near the private door, resolving when the pretended spectre advanced the next night, to follow and stab it with his sword; that his plan having succeeded, he immediately returned to the baron's mansion, and finding that every one was retired to rest, he had wandered about till the next morning, when he had assembled the vassals, and returned to the cavern with them, in the manner they had witnessed.

Father Francisco now entered the apartment, and informed them, that the baron had expired a few moments before in his arms. "Whatever may have been his faults heretofore," added the holy man, "he died a penitent, imploring that forgiveness, which God grant us all."

CHAPTER VIII

——Pale as the waning moon
With tear-stained cheek and stupid gaze,
Withering before life's sunny noon,
Grief crept along, in sad amaze,
By many a stroke to keenest misery brought,
Now in a show'r dissolv'd, now lost in inward thought.
PENROSE.

"OH! father," exclaimed Alphonso, "teach me how a sinner like myself can hope to be forgiven."

"Thy welfare in a future state shall be my care hereafter; already have I provided for thy safety in this world. The baron was moved by thy having preserved the life of his child, and according to his desire, I have already bound the vassals to secrecy, concerning the discovery of the cavern. After thou hast related thy unhappy story, and performed the last sad office which the baron has required of thee, thou must go with me to the monastery of Maqueda, and instantly take the vow which binds all those who live with us; *that* alone can save thee from the vengeance of offended justice; thy companions have joyfully accompanied father Benedict thither, whom, for thy sake, the baron has also spared."

Alphonso received this intelligence with the most grateful acknowledgements, and then spoke thus—"My real name is don Leon, of Seville. I was, in my youth, one of the most intimate companions of the deceased baron Garcia, and have passed many a night with him over accursed dice; when he set out for the holy wars, I was necessarily separated from him, but immediately on his return he invited me to his mansion, and we renewed our former course of life. About the time that the baroness, his wife, died, I had contracted with him an immense debt of honour, which I had no means of solving. I became melancholy; he perceived my dejection, and one day thus addressed me—'My dear Leon, does the small sum you are indebted to me cause your uneasiness? I fear it does, candidly answer me.' I told him, with the same frankness he had used towards me, that it did. He conjured me to think no more of it, expressed the greatest concern at my late want of spirits, and even forced me to accept no inconsiderable sum, to employ in a trial of regaining my fortune, which I had entirely lost. I made him every acknowledgement that words could convey, and never a day passed that I did not lament to him my inability to make him a more ample return; he told me, at length, that he could point out to me a way, by which I might entirely shake off the load of gratitude under which I, to his great concern, seemed to labour; I eagerly inquired it. He then, having sworn me to secrecy during his life, asked me to mix a powder in a goblet of wine, which I was to present to his brother Ferdinand, who was that night to visit him. Suffice it to say, my anxious desire to rid myself of the obligations under which it hurt my pride to continue, drove me on to do the deed, and curse myself. The poison I had administered was lingering, purposely prepared by the baron, to baffle suspicion. Twelve days after, Ferdinand died; I saw myself his murderer; his idea haunted me; my distracted imagination showed me my hands dyed in innocent blood; my nights and days were torture. To free myself from the recollection of one crime, I resolved to plunge into another of as black a dye. I entered the forest for the purpose of ending my own hated life, when two men, whom I by chance met, perceiving my situation, took me along with them, and endeavoured to deter me from the act they had seen me about to commit, by offering me a quiet abode, where they promised me that peace I could not hope for in the world. I suffered myself to be led by them to that fatal cavern. Left alone, I reflected on my situation; prayer and repentance stood forward as my kindest friends; I resolved to embrace them, and shuddering at the rash act I had been about to commit, I thanked my preservers for their care of me, and resolved to live amongst them; and they shortly after informed me of the mysteries of their abode. Upbraid me not," cried Alphonso, "I merit your pity; I have never yet been free from reproaches, more severe than words can frame—the stings of conscience."

His tears prevented his utterance. Henrico was affected by the agitation of his friend. Matilda held a hand of Altador and

Hypolita, and bathed them with the pearly drops that swiftly chased each other down her faded cheeks.

"I now come," continued Alphonso, after a short pause, "to the confession of the dying baron, which he desired me to make known to these friends after his death. He began by informing me, that the reason of his taking away his brother's life, was from a desire of espousing his widow, the beauteous Fatima, whom he was well assured, he could not hope by any other means to possess; that he had, by liberal donations, induced a friar, named father Paul, to persuade his brother on his death-bed, that he could not grant him absolution on any other terms than his bequeathing his entire possessions to Garcia, and that the credulous Ferdinand had accordingly signed a testament, drawn up by the treacherous friar; that immediately, on his brother's death, he had offered himself in marriage to Fatima, and that she had peremptorily refused him; upon which he had conceived the horrid design of immuring her in a secret apartment of the castle, which had before been known by his brother only, and then only by himself and father Paul, determining there to force her to compliance with his will; that the father had aided him in putting this scheme into execution, and that the miserable Fatima had ever since been confined there, where she had borne him a boy, which he had exposed in the forest, that child whom I fortunately saved from perishing."

"Mysterious Heaven!" exclaimed Hypolita, "why are the innocent thus plunged in misery—why do the guilty triumph?"

"Forbear to question that which Providence, in its all-wise direction, hides from mortal man," replied Francisco. "Learn from that unhappy sufferer," continued he, pointing to Alphonso, "that the innocent have a consoling friend, which ever denies its comforts to the wicked—the soothings of an approving conscience."

"Let us then hasten to restore her to liberty," cried Hypolita.

"I have not ended my account," said Alphonso; "the baron entreated me to say, that it was he himself who had so much alarmed the domestics, from the supposition of his being a spirit, as they had sometimes by chance seen him when he was going to the unhappy prisoner by night, to carry her such provisions and necessaries as she wanted; that Lopez was in all his secrets, and had attended Fatima during his late illness, and that he had usually sat up by night to warn him at his return, in case any one should be stirring in the mansion, and that this had been the case on the night of Villetta's alarm. He further told me that he had seen some one watching him that very night, as he retired to his chamber, but that the darkness of the place had prevented him from discovering who the person was, but that he imagined it to have been Jerome, from the alarm the old man had ever since testified at the mention of a spirit."

This supposition Altador confirmed. Alphonso had now finished his narration.

"Let us call Lopez, and proceed to the castle," said Francisco. Lopez entered the apartment.

He told them he had frequently bewailed the fate of the unhappy lady, but that he had sworn to keep the baron's secret, ere he knew what it was, and that his oath had prevented him from discovering what had constantly been a source of great uneasiness to him. He added also, that he believed the baron's sufferings had, at times, been great, as he had frequently returned from the castle with his eyes swollen with tears.

Hypolita conjured Matilda to endeavour to compose her agitated mind, and retire to her chamber, whilst they visited the castle, saying, that the scene they were going to witness would too greatly overpower her tender heart. Matilda felt the force of Hypolita's remark, and ascended to her chamber, attended by Flora, having dispatched two of her late father's vassals to the castle of Gonsalez, in search of her faithful Villetta.

In their way to the castle they met old Hugo, who expressed the most heartfelt joy at again seeing Altador, whom he had given up as lost. Altador, on his part, requested permission of his companions to inform him of what had happened, and expressed a wish of taking him with them to the castle; to this they readily agreed, knowing the old man's strong attachment to the youth.

Being arrived at the castle, Lopez opened the sliding panel; they passed through a dark passage, and entered a gloomy apartment—"This is the prison," said Lopez, pointing to a door facing them; he then unlocked and unbolted it; Hypolita pushed it gently open; what a scene presented itself to her view! The once beauteous Fatima, wasted to a skeleton, reclining her head on her emaciated arm, over which loosely hung a thin lock of hair, whitened by misfortune, not by age; her eyes, no longer vivid, but dimmed by never-ceasing tears, were fixed, half closed, upon the ground; she gently raised them, and seemingly insensible to all but grief, again hung down her head, nor uttered a single word. The lady Hypolita took her hand, but could not speak. Father Francisco broke the silence by telling her that her tyrant was no more, and that they were come to restore her to liberty.

"Give me death," she cried, in sounds scarcely articulate, "that were indeed a friend." A deep sigh followed; then starting up suddenly, she threw herself at Francisco's feet, and seizing his hand, exclaimed—"Where are my children?—where the darling boy I bore the monster in this dungeon?—That boy he tore from his fond mother's bosom."

"Receive him to thy arms," cried Alphonso.

Henrico fell on his mother's neck; she now raised her eyes, which gleamed with the wildness of frantic joy, clasped her hands, and sunk into the arms of Hypolita and Francisco.

The first ecstacies of maternal fondness being past, Alphonso informed her in what manner he had found Henrico, when about fifteen months old—"Oh! merciful God," exclaimed Fatima, "then he is not mine; the inhuman monster, Garcia, bereft me of my babe at three days old."

"Was this the mantle in which thy boy was exposed?" asked Alphonso, producing that in which he had found Henrico wrapt.

"Oh! no, no," returned Fatima, "unhappy that I am!" A flood of tears came to her relief.

"Oh! good father," cried Hugo, "that is a mantle that my Rosala was wont to wear; it was stolen from her on the very day the baron of Ollada's child that was at nurse with her died."

"If this be so," exclaimed Francisco, "that boy did never die, and thou, Fatima, art still a happy mother."

He then related the confession which Hugo's wife had made to him; Hugo himself particularized the time, and Fatima once more embraced him, as the offspring of her marriage bed—"My other boy," she cried, "I fear has perished; him his cruel father exposed in a cloak of leopard's skin."

"Then I fear he has indeed, lady," answered Hugo; "such a mantle I found some sixteen years back in back in this forest, but no child therewith."

"Oh! my dear lost boy," exclaimed Fatima; "but praised be Heaven that it hath not left me childless."

Fatima, at length, being somewhat composed, expressed her desire of being immediately conveyed to a neighbouring convent, where she wished to pass the remainder of her days in tranquillity, and where she could be frequently visited by her son, her niece Matilda, and those friends who now surrounded her, declaring her inability again to live in the world, after a seclusion of nineteen years.

According to her wish, they conveyed her thither, and delivered her to the care of a tender abbess, whose soothing attentions, aided by father Francisco's pious consolations, gradually lightened the grief which at times preyed on her mind, relative to the fate of her last-born infant.

Altador, in their return home, contrived to walk apart with Lopez, for the purpose of inquiring who the corpse was that he had seen in the closet of the kitchen in the castle, and Lopez informed him, that he had learnt from one of the duke's vassals, that it was one of his comrades that had been killed in the wood, adjoining the baron's mansion, by a young peasant, when he was, by Gaspero's commands, endeavouring to carry off Matilda; and that they had hid him there, lest, had they taken him back to the duke's castle, his death should have produced questions from the other vassals who were not in their master's confidence.

CHAPTER IX

Nor in his orisons let him forget
The hand of Heav'n, whose providential care
Has ordered all, the innocent to save,
To right the injur'd and reward the brave.
                                    CIBBER.

HENRICO, transported beyond himself at the recent discovery made by old Hugo, flew, with all the ardour of an impatient lover, to his idolized Matilda, and informed her of it. She received the intelligence with not less delight than he had communicated it; but the natural modesty of her sex taught her to give but faint utterance to the feelings of her heart, which she knew but ill how to suppress.

Altador, no longer beholding Henrico as a rival, now earnestly wished to see him the husband of Matilda, his sister, and taking her hand, joined it to that of Henrico, exclaiming—"As, noble youth, thou hast hitherto been made the peculiar instrument of Heaven, in defending my beloved sister, continue so to be; take her at a brother's hand, and mayest thou be as happy as thou art deserving."

Father Anselm and father Francisco fervently seconded the prayer, with eyes and hands uplifted to Heaven.

Henrico, now the declared heir of the Castle of Ollada, immediately ordered it to be repaired for the reception of himself and Matilda; and insisting that the lady Hypolita should not be separated from her amiable charge, apartments in the castle were set apart for her use.

The entrance to the cavern was closed up; but Henrico, at times, secretly revisited it, with mixed sensations of pleasure and sorrow; of pleasure, from the recollection of its having afforded him shelter in the helpless state of infancy; of sorrow, from the thought of its former disgraceful inhabitants.

Altador, having bestowed on Hugo and his daughter Jaquenetta, the small tenement and land they had before rented of Garcia, continued to reside in the mansion of his deceased father, retaining in his service the old steward, Perez, and the aged Jerome; and about a year after espoused Elvira, the daughter of donna Isabinda.

Villetta, happy in being again restored to Lopez, was soon after married to him, and received an advantageous vineyard in dower from her kind lady.

The unfortunate Fatima lived many years to enjoy the peaceful retreat in which her son had placed her; and when death at length called upon her, she met him with a firmness that bespoke her conscious rectitude of heart, and her faith in a benignant Providence.

Alphonso, already a penitent, comported himself in such a manner, as gained him the daily increasing esteem and friendship of the holy men amongst whom he lived.

Henrico and Matilda lived long and happily, esteemed by the affluent, beloved by the indigent, and revered by a numerous offspring, who resembled their excellent parents, not less in the noble qualities of an elevated mind, than in the conciliating graces of an engaging person.

FINIS.

NOTES

3   *epigraph:* John Home, *Douglas* (1756), Act V.
    Maqueda: a town in Spain near Toledo.
4   *St. Jago:* the patron saint of Spain, known in English as
    Saint James the Greater. The cry of "St. Jago" occurs fre-
    quently in Gothic novels set in Spain.
    plumes: the prattling of Hugo recalls the prattling of ser-
    vants in Horace Walpole's *The Castle of Otranto* (1764).
    The reference to "plumes" is a direct allusion to the giant
    plumed helmet which is found to have crushed Prince Con-
    rad in the opening scene of *Otranto.*
10 *epigraph:* Shakespeare, *All's Well that Ends Well,* I,i.
18 *epigraph:* John Dryden, *Oedipus,* I, i.
21 *a banditti:* Lathom, like many Gothic writers, uses the
    plural Italian "banditti," meaning bandits, as both a singular
    and a plural noun at various points in the novel.
23 *suit:* suite
25 *epigraph:* Matthew Prior, "Henry and Emma"
37 *epigraph:* John Milton, *Paradise Lost,* Book III
44 *her waiting-maid Villetta:* at least one contemporary critic
    praised Lathom's handling of the prating servant Villetta,
    which may appear odd to modern readers, since her inces-
    sant chattering seems to us today to be quite irritating.
55 *epigraph:* Shakespeare, *Coriolanus,* IV, iv.
65 *epigraphs:* Shakespeare, *The Merchant of Venice,* V, i, and
    A Midsummer Night's Dream, I, i.
73 *epigraph:* Shakespeare, *2 Henry VI,* III, ii.
76 *"rights which nature gave to all...":* Matilda's eloquent
    defence of women's natural rights is particularly interest-
    ing, as it comes from the pen of a male writer, and only
    three years after Mary Wollstonecraft's *A Vindication of
    the Rights of Women* (1792).
80 *Phoebus:* the Latin name for the Greek sun-god Apollo.
82 *epigraph:* Mark Akenside, "The Pleasures of Imagination"
    (1772).
84 *lupines:* plants of the genus *Lupin,* bearing erect spikes of
    usually purplish-blue flowers.
85 *wots:* knows
92 *epigraph:* Shakespeare, *As You Like It,* V, ii.
100 *epigraph:* Rev. Thomas Penrose, "The Hermit's Vision"

108   *epigraph:* Shakespeare, *Hamlet,* I, ii.

116   *tucket:* trumpet

116   *epigraph:* Shakespeare, *Othello,* I, iii.

132   *palmer:* a medieval European pilgrim who carried a palm branch as a token of having visited the Holy Land.

133   *epigraph:* Shakespeare, *Macbeth,* I, vii.

136   *cullies:* fools or dupes. The verb "to cully" meant "to cheat" or "to fool."

140   *epigraph:* Penrose, "The Hermit's Vision"

146   *epigraph:* Colley Cibber, *Ximena; or, the Heroick Daughter,* Act V

APPENDIX

Contemporary Reviews of *The Castle of Ollada*

The Castle of Ollada. A Romance. 2 volumes 12*mo.* 6*s. bound.*

Lane. 1795.

Another haunted castle! Surely the misses themselves must be tired of so many stories of ghosts, and murders,—though to the misses the ghosts of this novel present perhaps the most harmless part of the dramatis personæ. The heroine who could basely elope from her father's house with a young peasant whom she had only twice seen, and to whom she had scarcely ever spoken, is a personage of a far more pernicious nature. For though the heroine of a romance [is] always sure to know 'the true baron *upon instinct,*'—we do not think it altogether advisable for young ladies to put implicit confidence in such a conductor, and therefore cannot avoid reprobating the example.

— *The Critical Review,* July, 1795, p. 352.

The Castle of Ollada. A Romance. 12mo. 2 Vols. 6*s.* sewed.

Lane. 1795.

This performance is very properly entitled a Romance. The writer appears to have a fancy plentifully stored, from former romances, with images of love and terror, and a memory not ill furnished with the terms and phrases which belong to the school of fiction. The story, which is laid in Spain, tells of a beauteous damsel, the daughter of a haughty and cruel baron, whose charms enamour Henrico, a peasant of mysterious descent. Their moonlight interviews within a friendly grove; the hero's encounter, in a well-described tournament, with a wealthy duke to whom his mistress had been devoted; with sundry miscellaneous escapes and rescues; are in the true style of romance. Some of the inferior characters are well sketched, particularly that of the simple, credulous, prating Villetta, Matilda's waiting-woman. Had the writer confined himself to his love-tale, and opened it more at large by a fuller display of scenery, sentiment, and character, the performance would have been more complete: but, in order to gratify the fashionable taste, he has introduced a story of a castle supposed to be inhabited by ghosts, but at length discovered to be inhabited by a set of coiners; which will, we apprehend, afford the reader little amusement. We must add that the occupation of these coiners is represented in too favourable a light. The introduction of these incidents has increased the intricacy of the general story, and has obliged the writer to spend a great part of the second volume in explaining mysteries, which after all are not very clearly unfolded, when he ought to have been interesting the feelings of his readers in the fortune of his principal characters. The language is in general correct: but sometimes, in attempting to elevate his style, the writer falls into affected stateliness; for example, when he speaks of a horseman '*conceding* half his beast' to another person. The pointing is frequently inaccurate; in the very sentence of the book, the sense is concealed by a wrong use of the parenthesis. We mention these trifles because, notwithstanding the defects of this performance, we discern in it promising marks of ingenuity.

— *The Monthly Review,* October, 1795

WORKS BY FRANCIS LATHOM

The Castle of Ollada. A Romance. 2 vols. London: Minerva Press for William Lane, 1795. Second edition: London: A. K. Newman, 1831.
Modern editions: Seattle: Valancourt Books, 2005 (limited to 250 copies), Chicago: Valancourt Books, 2005 (second printing), Chicago: Valancourt Books, 2006 (new edition).

All in a Bustle. A Comedy in Five Acts. Norwich: Beatniffe and Payne, 1795. Second edition: Norwich: Printed for the author by J. Payne, 1800.

The Midnight Bell, a German Story, Founded on Incidents in Real Life. 3 vols. London: Printed for H. D. Symonds, 1798. Second edition: London: A. K. Newman, 1825.
Other editions: Dublin: N. Kelly, 1798 (2 vols.); Cork: Haly [etc.], 1798 (3 vols. in 1); Philadelphia: James Carey, 1799 (3 vols. in 1); Paris, 1799 [as *La Cloche de minuit*].
Modern editions: London: The Folio Press, 1968 (ed. Devendra P. Varma); London: Skoob Books, 1989 (ed. Lucien Jenkins).

Men and Manners. A Novel. 4 vols. London: Wright & Symonds, 1799. New edition: London: Printed by J. Davis for Wright & Symonds, 1800.
Other editions: Dublin: Burnet, 1799 (4 vols.)

Holiday Time, or The School Boy's Frolic: A Farce in Two Acts. Norwich: Printed for the author by J. Payne, 1800.

Orlando and Seraphina, or, The Funeral Pile. An Heroic Drama in Three Acts. London: Printed for the author and sold by Longman and Rees, [1800].

The Dash of the Day. A Comedy in Five Acts. Norwich: Printed for the author by J. Payne, 1800. Second edition: Norwich: Printed for the author by J. Payne, 1800. Third edition: Dublin: P. Wogan, 1801.

Mystery. A Novel. 2 vols. London: Symonds, 1800. Also published: Dublin: P. Wogan [etc.], 1800.

Curiosity. A Comedy in Three Acts. London: Printed by J. Parslee for T. Hurst, 1801.

Astonishment!!! A Romance of a Century Ago. 2 vols. London: Printed for T. N. Longman and O. Rees [by J. Payne, Norwich], 1802.
Second edition: London: A. K. Newman, 1821.

Erestina. A Tale Taken from the French. Norwich: Payne [1803?]

The Wife of a Million: a Comedy in Five Acts. Norwich: Printed and sold by J. Payne for Longman and Rees, 1803.

Very Strange, but Very True! or, The History of an Old Man's Young Wife. 4 vols. London: Longman and Rees, 1803.
Second edition: London: A. K. Newman, 1821.

The Castle of the Tuileries: or, a Narrative of All the Events Which Have Taken Place in the Interior of that Palace, from the Time of its Construction to the Eighteenth Brumaire of the Year VIII. Translated from the French. 2 vols. London: Longman and Rees, 1803.

The Impenetrable Secret, Find it Out! A Novel. 2 vols. London: Printed at the Minerva Press for Lane, Newman, and Co., 1805. Second edition: London: A. K. Newman, 1831.

The Mysterious Freebooter, or The Days of Queen Bess. A Romance. 4 vols. London: Minerva Press for Lane, Newman, and Co., 1806.
Other editions: London: Jaques and Wright, 1818 [New ed., 4 vols. in 1]; London: Jaques and Wright, 1829 (4 vols. in 1); London: W. J. White, 1844 (as *The Mysterious Freebooter; or, The Bride of Mystery*).

The Fatal Vow, or St. Michael's Monastery. 2 vols. London: Crosby, 1807.

Human Beings. A Novel. 3 vols. London: Crosby, 1807.

The Unknown; or, The Northern Gallery. A Romance. 2 vols. London: Minerva Press for Lane, Newman, and Co., 1808. Second edition: London: A. K. Newman, 1826. Other editions: Paris: Dentu, 1810, 5 vols. [as *L'inconnu, ou, la Galerie mystérieuse*].

London; or, Truth Without Treason. 4 vols. London: Minerva Press for Lane, Newman, and Co., 1809.

The Romance of the Hebrides, or, Wonders Never Cease! 3 vols. London: Minerva Press for A. K. Newman and Co., 1809.

Italian Mysteries, or, More Secrets Than One. 3 vols. London: Minerva Press for A. K. Newman and Co., 1820. Other editions: Paris, 1823, 3 vols. [as *Les Mystères Italiens, ou Le Château della Torrida*].

The One-Pound Note and Other Tales. 2 vols. London: A. K. Newman, 1820. Modern edition: Chicago: Valancourt Books, 2006 (forthcoming)

Puzzled and Pleased; or, The Two Old Soldiers and Other Tales. 3 vols. London: A. K. Newman, 1822.

Live and Learn; or, The First John Brown, His Friends, Enemies, and Acquaintance, in Town and Country. A Novel. 4 vols. London: A. K. Newman, 1823.

The Polish Bandit; or, Who is My Bride? and Other Tales. 3 vols. London: A. K. Newman, 1824.

Young John Bull; or, Born Abroad and Bred at Home. A Novel. 3 vols. London: A. K. Newman, 1828.

Fashionable Mysteries; or, The Rival Duchesses and Other Tales. 3 vols. London: A. K. Newman, 1829.

Mystic Events; or, The Vision of the Tapestry. A Romantic Legend of the Days of Anne Boleyn. 4 vols. London: A. K. Newman, 1830.

ABOUT FRANCIS LATHOM[*]

Jenkins, James D. "Introduction" to *Italian Mysteries.* Chicago: Valancourt Books, 2005.

Jenkins, Lucien. "Introduction" to *The Midnight Bell.* London: Skoob Books, 1989.

MacConochie, Arthur A. *Francis Lathom: Forgotten Goth.* [Charlottesville, Va.], 1949 (unpublished master's thesis).

Nause, John. *The Eclipsed Orb: a Study of Francis Lathom, His Life, Gothic Romances, Plays and Experiments in Forms of Fiction.* Halifax: Department of English, Dalhousie University, 1987.

Potter, Franz J. *The History of Gothic Publishing, 1800-1835.* Basingstoke: Palgrave Macmillan, 2005.

Punter, David and Alan Bissett. "Francis Lathom in the Eighteenth Century," *Gothic Studies* 5: 1 (2003), 55-70.

Summers, Montague. *The Gothic Quest.* London: The Fortune Press, [1938] (Rpt. New York: Russell & Russell: 1964).

Varma, Devendra P. "Introduction" to *The Midnight Bell.* London: The Folio Press, 1968.

---

[*] Only recently, through the separate researches of the present editor and Franz Potter, have accurate details of Francis Lathom's life begun to emerge. Thus, while the works listed here contain useful information with regard to Lathom's work, they should not be counted upon with regard to biographical information.

ALSO BY FRANCIS LATHOM

Italian Mysteries

"He drew aside the covering which concealed the face of the subject...guess, if you can, the horror, the astonishment, when, in the countenance of the deceased, I beheld my own mother!"

The worthy doctor Urbino di Cavetti is kidnapped and led blindfolded to the bedside of a young woman. A mysterious nobleman offers him an immense fortune if he will consent to cure her...of her life! Horrified, Urbino refuses to murder her, and must flee his native Venice with his family to avoid the powerful stranger's vengeance.

They flee to the isolated Castello della Torvida, which local peasants affirm to be haunted. But the spectre the servants see and the supernatural warnings the family receives are the least of their worries when Urbino's niece, the lovely Paulina, is kidnapped by the lascivious Marchese di Valdetti.

Confined a prisoner in Valdetti's castle, Paulina must choose: become the Marchese's wife, or fall victim to his insatiable lust! Can her friends penetrate the mysteries of the haunted castle and save Paulina in time?

With a colourful cast of characters and an intricate plot, *Italian Mysteries* was among Francis Lathom's most successful Gothic novels. This edition, the first since 1820, includes a new introduction and explanatory notes for modern readers.

ISBN 0-9766048-6-8
Trade Paperback, 5.5" x 8.5"
408pp, July 2005, $17.95